Parktails

Parktails

DOUGLAS G. CAMPBELL

RESOURCE *Publications* • Eugene, Oregon

PARKTAILS

Resource Publications
An Imprint of Wipf and Stock Publishers
199 W. 8th Ave., Suite 3
Eugene, OR 97401
www.wipfandstock.com

ISBN 13: 978-1-61097-820-0
Manufactured in the U.S.A.

This tale is dedicated to my sons Joshua and Ian.

Contents

Acknowledgments

ALL BOOKS have input other than that of the stated author, so I thank Malcolm R. Campbell, Lesa Campbell, and Rebecca Propst for reading my manuscript, making editorial suggestions, and assisting with proofreading. I thank my two sons Joshua and Ian for giving me the impetus to think about and then write this story. I thank my wife Rebecca for playful banter about animals and their working conditions in national parks, before any words were put on paper.

Critters List

(cast of major characters)

Alexia: a female grizzly bear and Geyser District sheriff

Arachanar: an ancient female spider

Blinkers: a male raccoon, Geyser District secretary, and the narrator

Brogoff: a male bear

Bugler: a large male elk

Cawalla Pan: a male antelope

Cawdor: a male crow

Dozema: a female skunk

Gondzor: a male Canada goose and Geyser District assistant ranger

Grimla: a male mountain lion

Keeble: a female deer

Mendacitus: a large male serpent

Menki: a female eagle

Morgorgor: a wise old female porcupine

Pabatackle: a playful male otter

Quququic: a female warbler

Rittiticket: a male ground squirrel

Romla: a female mountain lion

Rutorina: a female skunk.

Skeezer: old male skunk

Tennial: a male bison and Geyser District deputy sheriff

Thimblewicket: a female ground squirrel

Tromengard: a female moose and Udena's mother

Udena: a young female moose and Tromengard's daughter

Wanda: a female moth

Zeecor Manata: a male antelope

Zornova: a female bison and Geyser District ranger

Business as Usual?

TROMENGARD WAS on the phone again. Tromengard was so angry it was difficult to understand what she was saying. However, I was able to understand that Thimblewicket, the dispatcher had sent her, no doubt by mistake to a wooded area that was just the worst smoldering blackened mess. "Udena, my daughter and me . . . well I am just livid. I want that crack-brained Thimblewicket to apologize at once. To think that he would send us into a holocaust like that, a wretched smoke-blackened desert, and just after we had taken our morning bath. Gondzor! Gondzor, are you listening to me?"

"Yes, Tromengard, I'm listening," answered Gondzor, with a sigh, for it had not been a good day. "I will certainly register your complaint and Thimblewicket will be reprimanded if she is to blame. And Tromengard, I am sorry Udena suffered so much from the smoke. I know how delicate and sensitive she is."

"You can hem and haw all you like, Gondzar," grumbled Tromengard, "but I am furious. So don't think you can get away with a mere reprimand. I want Thimblewicket fired!" Apparently Tromengard had slammed down the phone, for Gondzor flinched before he hung up the phone.

Oh it was just a terrible day. And it wasn't really Thimblewicket's fault. The scouting reports from the district had been less than adequate since Jet and Cruise were both molting. Jet and Cruise, both red-shouldered hawks, are our best scouts. Some days the Geyser District of the park is just so frazzling that it doesn't pay to come to work. And Tromengard can be so unpleasant and haughty, even though Gondzor, my boss, is so kind and patient. Oh I do so admire our district's assistant ranger.

Now look at what I've done. I've got you all confused no doubt. Perhaps I should sit down and slow down. I know what I will do. I'll take a deep breath, to calm myself. Aaaaaah. Uuuuuuh. There, that did help. I suppose that I should introduce myself. I'm Blinkers, Gondzor's secretary, here at the Geyser District office. I'm the secretary because of my nimble fingers, I'm a raccoon you know, and because I am so fastidious. I am fastidious about my work too. Everything should be put in the right file, all words should be spelled correctly and my life would be so much easier if all the paperwork was turned in according to schedule. Tromengard, for example, is always late with her travel vouchers. But I guess you must expect that from a moose. She says the vouchers are late because Udena is so delicate and needs attention every moment of the day. Udena weighs a delicate 400 pounds even though she isn't yet a year old, delicate—well really!

Oh my, oh my, I am as jittery as a crawfish. I'll take another breath. Aaaaaaah. Uuuuuuh. Buzzzzzzzz!

"Yes, Gondzor, I'll come right in . . . yes I'll bring you the labor relations file." Bugler the elk and Tromengard have been agitating for higher wages and shorter hours for all ungulates in the district. They want more vacation time too.

Gondzor spends most of his time in the small pool in his office when he's at work. It's not really unusual; he's a Canada goose. We work well together, though he does get grumpy when I wash my food in his pool. Now that's something I've never understood. "Gondzor, here you are; these are the files you wanted."

"Yes, thank you Blinkers. Remember you must be at tonight's meeting to take the minutes," Gondzor replied.

"Oh yes, you can rely on me, Gondzor. Will Zornova be there too?" Zornova is our District Ranger; she's a bison.

"Yes, she should return from Falls District in time for the meeting. You can depend on Zornova" Gondzor responded, as he began to turn the pages of the report with his left wing. Most Canada Geese are left-winged, you know.

The afternoon zipped by in a blur of activity. So after a quick meal I raced to the meeting. Oh, it was a regular knock and tumble session, that meeting was. The ungulates began chanting even before Gondzor arrived "give Thimblewicket the hoof! Send Thimblewicket to beg for tourists' peanuts!" Poor Thimblewicket was so agitated that she kept running her tail through her forepaws as she sat with the other rodents in the balcony. The small rodents always sit in the balcony to avoid being trod upon.

As soon as Zornova, who had arrived in time, called the meeting to order Bugler demanded to be heard. "Yes Bugler, you may have your say. But come to the point and keep your voice down, I warn you, or I will have you thrown out on your antler." Zornova would not be cowed by Bugler, one of the largest bull elk in the park.

So Bugler spoke for the ungulates, or at least many of them, "I tell you, Madam Ranger, we ungulates are the chief draw of the park. It is for us that the tourists come to Geyser District. It is to see our proud and majestic physiques and to take pictures of us with their cameras that they travel here from all over the country, from all parts of the world. I must tell you that we large ungulates bear the brunt of the workload. We must hoof it all over the district to be in meadow number twenty-three by dawn then we are expected to prance over to field number seventy-three until sunset."

"Yes, Bugler's right; too much is expected of us. Grimla, Romla, and the other mountain lions don't have to put up with such a schedule. And then that tourist-brained Thimblewicket sends Udena, with her delicate lungs, and me into the midst of a blazing inferno!" interjected Tromengard.

Zornova, banging her hoof on the floor brought the meeting to order again, and just in time, for a chorus of high-pitched shrieking was issuing from the balcony. "Tromengard," threatened

Zornova, "you must wait your turn like everyone else. Now be silent or I will ask you to leave."

Tromengard moved back, but then lay down on the floor in a sulk. Bugler continued, "we demand a ten percent pay increase, a six hour day, and a three week summer vacation for all the larger ungulates. If we don't get what we demand then we will not work, we will call a strike!" Most of the larger ungulates rumbled their hooves on the floor, signifying their approval.

"Madam Ranger! Madam Ranger! I protest, I protest," squeaked forth the voice of Thimblewicket, the golden-mantled ground squirrel. "These large ungulates always demand too much. They think they are all that the people come to see! I've had it up to my forepaws with their regal insolence. I move that we reject their request, and reject it immediately!"

Zornova responded, "Thank you for your views Thimblewicket, this is not the first time you have expressed them. Morgorgor you may now speak your mind. All the animals spread apart creating a wide opening as Morgorgor the porcupine shambled forward. They sought to avoid her sharp quills.

"Madam Ranger," Morgorgor began "I move that you appoint a special committee to consider Bugler's request."

At this point Pabatackle, who had been spitting pinecone seeds at various animals in the audience shouted, "I second Morgorgor's motion and request an end to this boring meeting."

After the motion passed Thimblewicket and Zornova selected a committee made up of Morgorgor the porcupine, Pabatackle the otter, Rittiticket the ground squirrel, Romla the mountain lion, Keeble the mule deer, Brogoff the black bear, Qububquic the warbler, and me Blinkers the raccoon, to make recommendations on wages, hours, and benefits. Zornova left us with the admonition. "Summer will soon be here and we cannot afford to have a strike after two years of strikes by the bison, antelope, and eagles. We must come up with a solution and we must do it quickly." The committee was directed to report back within two weeks.

"Madam Ranger I object!" shouted Bugler. "There is no reason why we should wait so long for a silly report, when it is inevitable that we ungulates shall be vindicated and our request granted."

"Silence!" thundered Zornova, "I warned you not to raise your voice Bugler. If you continue to shout, you will be thrown out."

Bugler raised his antlers high above the crowd but did not speak, for he along with the others present glanced toward Alexia, the grizzly and the bison Tennial, the district sheriff and her deputy. Bugler, though puffed with pride, knew better than to confront Alexia.

Before any further fuel could be thrown into the heated meeting there was a sudden clamor. Cawdor, the raven, swooped down before those assembled and landed in front of Zornova and the unflappable Gondzor.

"Oh my, oh my, it's such a tragedy! Oh horror, horror, horror, horror, horror, what a black day this is! This day will long be remembered as a day of infamy, incredible infamy!" jabbered the almost incoherent Cawdor.

"Cawdor calm yourself!" ordered Zornova.

"Do take a deep breath and then relay your message," interjected Gondzor, in his most soothing deep voice.

Cawdor took a deep breath, but before he could speak he toppled over and fainted into a heap of black feathers. It was then that Wanda, who had followed Cawdor in through the upper window, flitted forward. In the midst of the present commotion no one had noticed the entrance of the diminutive Wanda, the brown moth.

"Madam Ranger," said the sedate moth "may I be allowed to continue where Cawdor left off in his report?"

Yes Wanda, please put an end to our deep curiosity," answered Zornova.

"Cawdor is correct," said Wanda "there has been a great tragedy. A bus struck Dozema the skunk, and she is dead. Cawdor and I were on duty near meadow sixteen, where highway seventy-three crosses the river. Several of the deer were grazing nearby, so cars full of tourists had stopped by the roadside."

"A people family got out of their car to take pictures of the deer, Freckles, Gambit, Swasher, and little Thicket, I believe," Wanda continued. "While the two parents were taking pictures their small daughter wandered out into the highway, following Gimlet the butterfly; Gimlet had inadvertently caught her attention. At that moment a large bus came around the curve, and apparently the driver did not notice the child in the road, for he did not slow the bus to a stop."

"Dozema, who had been eating pine nuts on the far side of the highway, was the only one paying attention. She knew that the little girl would be killed if she did not act. To save the child she ran towards the girl hissing and squeaking in a threatening manner. The frightened child turned and ran quickly back to her parents and out of the bus's path. But Dozema was hit by the left front tire and tossed into the gravel by the side of the road."

"The tourists left quickly; all were complaining of the bad smell. A man from another car, who had turned around in time to see Dozema's heroic act, remarked to his wife as he got back in the car, 'I didn't know that skunks ever became rabid; how fortunate for the child that the beast was hit by the bus. What a stink, we've got to get out of here quickly!'"

A hush had fallen over those assembled for the meeting, as Wanda told her sad tale. Even Bugler let his proud neck droop; tears began to fall from many eyes. When Wanda finished her story Morgorgor shambled forward. "Madam Ranger," said Morgorgor, "I move that we take a moment of silence to reflect on Dozema's heroic and costly sacrifice."

All of the assembled murmured their agreement. Silence descended upon the gathering, even Pabatackle stopped spiting pinecone seeds at Tromengard and wept quietly. Several minutes later Morgorgor spoke again. "Madam Ranger, I move that we bring this meeting to a close, for we can hardly continue a meeting at a time of such sadness. I humbly beg that you, Zornova, be the one to deliver the eulogy at Dozema's funeral. Further, I request that Bugler be put in charge of the celebration of joy following the funeral services."

Zornova, seeing that almost everyone was in agreement, declared the meeting closed and announced that the funeral would take place in two days at Stony Burrow. Although the uproar of the meeting had subsided there was a great deal of tension in the air as the ungulates stalked out. Angry eyes stared down from the balcony where the rodents were assembled.

Oh, I've been so people-brained tonight! My notes are such a mess, how will I ever get the minutes written? And tomorrow I will have to meet with the committee to discuss the ungulates' demands. Oh, I shall be up all night in front of the computer.

The Committee Meeting

WHEN THE sun rose the next morning the forest was soggy and the sky was gray with drizzle. I quickly gathered up my notebook, pencils, and my other secretarial accouterments, and placed them in my attaché case; then I rushed through the chill of morning in order to arrive punctually. My fur was absolutely soaked by the time I reached the appointed meeting site, so I groomed myself as I waited for the others to arrive. I was the first one to reach the rock overhang where the committee was to meet. I was early for I believe that one should never be late—never be late! To be late is rude, or so I say. I opened my attaché case and took out my writing pad and pencil so I would be ready.

Morgorgor soon ambled up through the tall wet grass, shook her whole body to dry herself, and then sat down by the end of a log. Romla came next, followed not long afterward by Brogoff the black bear. They both lay down near the rock wall, back among the shadows. Thimblewicket raced under the overhang, but tripped over a pinecone near the entrance and went tumbling across the dirt floor, narrowly missing Morgorgor's sharp quills. Quququic flew in next. Keeble entered gracefully and quietly, almost without being noticed.

We were chatting away with each other when Brogoff growled, "Where is that silly Pabatackle? Why must he always be late?"

Keeble answered "Don't be such a grump Brogoff, you know how Pabatackle likes a wet day like today. He probably got sidetracked chasing frogs down by Croaker's Pond."

"Well," Morgorgor said with great deliberation, "perhaps we should begin without him, he knew when the meeting was to begin."

Romla suggested that we put the matter to a vote, and all of us agreed to start the meeting without Pabatackle.

Almost immediately Thimblewicket chirped up, "I nominate Keeble to chair the meeting!"

Romla seconded the motion and everyone else agreed, so the meeting began.

"Blinkers, have you got the files on hours, wages, and vacations?" asked Keeble.

"Yes, oh yes I do, and may I point out that I have studied the figures. I have compared the figures. We must consider the importance, the relevance of all these statistics. These statistics are most important, most important," I answered.

"Will you please just stick to the numbers? Just give us the figures on weekly hours worked," Keeble replied.

"Oh yes, oh yes, I most certainly will. I will stick to the facts; facts are what we need to know. Now let me see, let me check my notes. Oh yes, let me find page fourteen; page fourteen has what we need to know. Here it is; I've found the numbers we need. Average working hours for ungulates per week is 32.7; average hours for small rodents is 43.2, and for large rodents 41.6. Felines average 25.3 hours, canidae 38.7, raptors 34.8, woodpeckers 39.5—the list goes on and on you see—it goes on and on," I said.

"Could you give us a summary, a very, very brief summary?" Keeble asked.

Though I detected a hint of sarcasm in Keeble's voice, I provided the requested summary. "Well yes I will do that; I will be very brief, very concise and to the point, I will not stray one small step from the facts. Let me see, here it is, here are the averages of hours worked for all animals of the Geyser District. On average we work 38.2 hours per week during the summer tourist season. Though I must say that Gondzor averages 53.9, and Zornova averages 52.1 hours per week, very dedicated those two are. Though I would not want to brag, I must say that I average 75.1 one hours per week. It's all that computer work, so much time spent in front of the computer." I would have continued to outline the facts, but Keeble interrupted me.

"Thank you, Blinkers, for the facts," responded Keeble. "Can the committee make a recommendation on a reduction in hours for ungulates?"

Brogoff was about to speak when the damp air was split in two with cries of high-pitched laughter. All of a sudden Pabatackle came sliding through the wet grass on the steep bank opposite the overhang. A small mound functioned like a ramps sending Pabatackle flying through the air. Pabatackle giggling with delight throughout his slide and flight, landed with a soft thump against Brogoff's fury side. Doubling up with laughter, Pabatackle rolled into Morgorgor's quills. A pain-filled and pitiful whine filled the ears of all those at the meeting, and all those within several miles, no doubt.

"I'm skewered, I've been made into a shish kebob," whimpered the deflated otter.

All of us held our bellies and covered our mouths with our paws, except for Keeble and Qququic, who had no paws, just to keep from laughing. Thimblewicket, though she tried, could not contain herself and burst into a high-pitched squeaking laugh. Pabatackle was about to swat the small rodent with his forepaw, when he heard a warning growl from above. He looked up, only to find Romla standing over him, her tail twitching back and forth in a menacing way.

It did not take Qququic long to pull two sharp quills from Pabatackle's rear end. Though Pabatackle moaned pathetically for a while, he soon returned to his silly old ways. His pain soon forgotten, once it no longer brought him any attention, he began decorating Morgorgor's quills with wild strawberries.

"We are so pleased you were able to attend this meeting young Pabatackle," intoned the ever calm Keeble. "All of us are so sorry that this meeting was not set at a convenient time for you. You are such a very busy otter, with all those frogs to chase, and wet hillsides to slide upon," she continued. "Now, Brogoff you were about to speak."

Brogoff, who spoke with a very deep voice, said, "It seems to me that the ungulates have no room to complain about the hours they work. Nor do the annual travel to stride figures show that they cover more distance in an average week that the rest of us."

"Oh, I agree with Brogoff, let the record show that we all most definitely and completely reject the wage proposal of the ungulates. Down with ungulates, down with the ungulates I say, drive them from the park I say!" squeaked Thimblewicket.

She stopped and shrank back with embarrassment when Quququic cheeped softly into her ear, "Be quiet you silly ground squirrel, Keeble is an ungulate, remember that Keeble is an ungulate. And so is Zornova!"

With a somewhat subdued and repentant tone Thimblewicket spoke again "Keeble, I am so embarrassed; I'm so sorry that I got carried away. I did not mean to insult you, for I have always respected you, and I know that you work hard."

"Apology accepted," replied the magnanimous mule deer.

Our committee meeting continued almost until noon. In the end we decided that the ungulates had no basis for their request for higher wages (more feed) for their summer work. We thought that they might indeed deserve higher wages in the winter. In winter the ground was covered with snow, and unlike many of us, they could not hibernate or sleep through much of the winter. Further, we recommended no change in the number of hours worked. Since no animals were allowed any except emergency vacations in the summer, we saw no reason why ungulates should have a summer vacation. However, since ungulates had to work for the winter tourists as well, we thought consideration should be given to a plan that would allow more vacation time in the spring or fall.

Once the meeting had ended Pabatackle was soon rollicking through the wet grass, the sharp prick of Morgorgor's quills apparently forgotten. Brogoff frowned reprovingly at the silly otter as he shambled among the trees overturning logs and stones as he searched for nuts.

The fact that I had more minutes to prepare dominated my thinking. Oh, I shall be up all night and tomorrow my paws will be ever so sore. A secretary's work is never done. Oh I have no desire for attention, I want no glory. I'm not the only one who has work to do. Yet if anyone needs a vacation, it's me. I thought to myself as I neatly re-filed my papers and returned folders to my attaché case, one must be fastidious, ever fastidious or the whole district would descend into anarchy. Yes, everything must be put in its proper place, that's what I say.

Dozema's Funeral

Each species has its own funeral customs. Coyotes sing sorrowful laments at sunset, bison conduct ritual stampedes, and eagles circle high into the clouds above. Skunks are a somber lot, so they are not given to elaborate public demonstrations of grief. Dozema's body had already been placed on a flat stone high above in Willow Meadow, just below Spiny Ridge, not more than a hundred yards from Stony Burrow. I for one was happy that the wind was coming from the south, so the odor of the deceased was blown away from the assembled crowd in Willow Meadow. Willow Meadow is not easy to get to, you seldom see people there since it is far from any trail or path. It is ideally suited for large gatherings because of its size and privacy. Hundred of animals had already arrived and more were emerging from the nearby forest. Tourists would complain today that wildlife was non-existent, but that was not true. Several squads of deer, ground squirrels, and others were at the most popular tourist sites.

Each species has its own way of showing respect for the dead. Zornova and the bison Tennial were caked with mud, for it was their custom to roll in a muddy bog in preparation for a funeral. Cawdor, along with the other ravens cried loudly from the tops of tall firs. Their dissonant laments cast a somber pall across the meadow and surrounding ridges. Wanda flitted about the meadow flowers until she was exhausted and landed on the uncomfortable thorns of a thistle pod, in the manner of grieving moths. As you may know raccoons, to honor the dead, sit still as though they were statues carved from stone. This is extremely difficult for raccoons. We always feel better when we are in motion; long periods of stillness lead to discomfort.

Skeezer, the oldest of the skunks, gave a shrill whistle; the ravens ceased their atonal dies ire, moths settled on thistle pods, and movement ceased; it was time for the ceremony. Soon stillness and quiet reigned in Willow Meadow and we were ready to begin.

For what seemed like hours, but was less than fifteen minutes, all of the animals assembled stopped moving and became respectfully quiet. Rutorina, Dozema's daughter, began whistling an eerie and haunting dirge. Next, Zornova paced slowly up to a small hillock. She stared out over the crowd of animals filling the meadow, and she began her brief eulogy.

> Dozema, the star dancer,
> looks down upon us now
> to give us the answer.
> She knows now the life
> after dark life, dark death
> after duty and daily strife.
> We too will also travel
> to the life that follows
> death upon the roadside gravel.
> Dozema, the star dancer,
> who saved the child
> gives us the answer.

At the end of the eulogy all the birds flew up into the air. Each cried out creating a raucous cacophony of high-pitched sounds that enveloped us as it descended earthward. Small rodents, the ground squirrels, mice, and prairie dogs, skittered about in nervous and frenetic dances of jubilation until they fell exhausted upon the grassy field. The ungulates circled about the meadow five times then trailed out of Willow Meadow towards Shooting Star Meadow, where the celebration of joy would soon begin.

As the ungulates began to circle we noticed the smell of smoke. A few minutes later roiling, black, ash-laden smoke began to drift over the meadow. It was indeed a black day. As soon as Zornova stepped down from the hillock and the funeral was over Gondzor landed, for he had risen up with the other birds.

"Zornova!" cried Gondzor, "a vast fire is approaching. Right now it is coming slowly from the north, but as the wind picks up this afternoon it will gain speed. I have sent Quququic and the others to warn all those who live throughout the Geyser District. Jet has flown back to headquarters to inform Thimblewicket of the approaching danger. Thimblewicket has been instructed to find out as much as she can from other districts and Cruise will return soon with a long range scouting report."

"Very good Gondzor," replied Zornova. "Blinkers, stop wringing your paws. I need you to write messages to be sent to those in danger. Gondzor, I will head for the Geyser District Ranger Station; I want you to take charge in the outlying districts to the north since you can spread the word more quickly than I. Also, since the fire has already reached the northern part of the district you can take charge of the injured. Tennial can take charge of the east. Alexia, you can take charge of the west. Keeble, since you are also swift, you shall warn those who live in the path of the fire."

Cruise, no longer molting, flew towards us just as Zornova completed her instructions. He reported that the fire extended over several thousand acres between the river and the highway. Zornova quickly dispatched her staff. Then, just as quickly, she dictated several messages for Menki, the eagle, to deliver to other district rangers. By the time Zornova had finished, the sky was almost completely black with smoke. It was time to leave.

Zornova stepped back up onto the hillock and bellowed for quiet, then she said "All of us must flee from this fire. All of you follow Keeble over Fir Cone ridge, and then keep going down the opposite slope towards the ranger station. Larger animals must give smaller and slower animals rides on their backs. Remain calm;

there is plenty of time for all of us to escape to safety. We can stay ahead of the fire if we remain calm, if we don't lose our heads."

Zornova moved away from the hillock and began directing various animals to help each other. All who had come for Dozema's funeral in Willow Meadow were soon moving towards Fir Cone Ridge in an orderly manner.

"Get up on my Back Blinkers, Zornova ordered, "we need to get to headquarters quickly."

Soon I was bumping along while holding on to Zornova's thick fur. I have never liked bison-back riding, but I've had to do it on several occasions when dire emergencies occurred. Three years ago, for instance, the bison Tennial fell into a mud hole and could not get out. Zornova raced to the scene with me holding onto her fur as tightly as I could. Then Zornova demonstrated that she could be quite resourceful. She shoved a log over to the edge of the mud hole with her head. Then I had to walk out on the log, tie the rope around both of Tennial's horns and then walk back along the log. All was going well until Tennial lurched while I was on the log and I went flying up into the air, then splat right into the mud. Fortunately for me I landed near the edge, so I scrabbled out without assistance. Well I thought my fur would never be the same after that. Oh how was I ever going to wash out that sulfurous slime? Well anyway, Zornova pulled Tennial out, though it did take some time, for Tennial is a large bison.

"Blinkers, you can climb down now," Zornova repeated.

Oh me, I must have closed my eyes again. I often do that when I go bison-back riding. I close my eyes so I won't think about falling off. And when I close my eyes I don't pay attention any more. And it has happened again, and Zornova is standing patiently in front of the Geyser District headquarters, waiting for me to climb down from her back. Oh I am such a scaredy-tourist. I am surely no thrill seeker, not me.

I followed Zornova up the steps, through the outer office into her large office. Though bison, in general, are afraid of fire (they tend to stampede), Zornova maintained her calm demeanor. She stood behind a large table scanning the reports scattered over most of its surface.

"Blinkers," she said, "go check with Thimblewicket to find out if any new reports have come in since these arrived. Also, see if you can find Rittiticket so he can help Thimblewicket with the flurry of dispatches," she added.

"Yes Zornova, I will certainly do that, I will check with Thimblewicket, I will find Rittiticket to help Thimblewicket. I will do all of what you say right away; I will do it this very instant, I will get right on it . . ."

"Blinkers!" Zornova bellowed.

She seldom roared. What could have put her out of sorts I wonder?

"Yes, Zornova," I replied, trying not to let on how hurt I was that she had bellowed at me. "What do you want?"

"Blinkers you seem to be standing still when we have many urgent demands upon us." Zornova spoke much more calmly now.

"Yes Zornova." I had almost forgotten about the fire, Thimblewicket, Rittiticket and all that. I had not realized that I was wringing my paws again and that my feet had not moved even one inch closer to the door. "Oh, I am so sorry, I must apologize Zornova. I am so ashamed of myself, at a time like this, for acting as though my feet are nailed to the floor like I have."

"Blinkers!"

I was finally able to move and I soon found that my legs had taken me down the hall to dispatch central. Thimblewicket thrust a paw full of hastily scribbled messages at me through an open window, then slammed down the window and continued writing furiously. I went straight back to Zornova's office and laid the messages out carefully in the order that they had arrived. Oh, but they were such a mess of scribbles. This will never do, I said to myself, I must make up a memo about penanimalship for the office staff. Really there is no excuse for such messy writing. As I was mentally composing my memo on penanimalship I hurried back out of the headquarters building, across the open yard in front of the district headquarters towards Rittiticket's tree stump.

"Rittiticket, are you home? Rittiticket! Oh Rittiticket wake up and come out here!" I shouted down his hole as loudly as I could.

Soon a grumpy, sleepy-eyed Rittiticket peered out into the bright, though quickly darkening, day

"What's the ruckus? What's all this yelling and shouting about? I say Blinkers, you had best mind your manners or I'll file a complaint. Just because you are district secretary—well you have no special rights," he sputtered.

"Rittiticket, do be quiet," I snapped self-righteously. "This is an emergency. There is no time at all for complaints and making nasty faces like that. Zornova sent me to fetch you. You must come help Thimblewicket, for there is a great fire and she is being overwhelmed with dispatches; you should just see the awful scribbling she has sent Zornova. Really there is no excuse for such poor penanimalship."

But before I could finish all that I had to say Rittiticket had skittered past me, as fast as he could, towards the district headquarters. Meanwhile the sky had become blacker and ash was beginning to drift down from above. Deer, porcupines, bison, elk, ground squirrels, and others were engaged in a flurry of activity. Pudge, the marmot, was busy tying shovel attachments to the hooves of bison and elk. These bison and elk would attempt to dig a shallow trench to stop the fire. Deer were packed with top priority files from the ranger headquarters and sent on their way to a temporary headquarters. We had just learned that a wind shift had occurred; we were now directly in the path of the surging, uncoiling flames. Squirrels and jays were sent to hurry the evacuation of the immediate vicinity, to warn all of the forest dwellers that they must leave at once. Soon though, I was back at my desk writing messages that Zornova was dictating over the intercom.

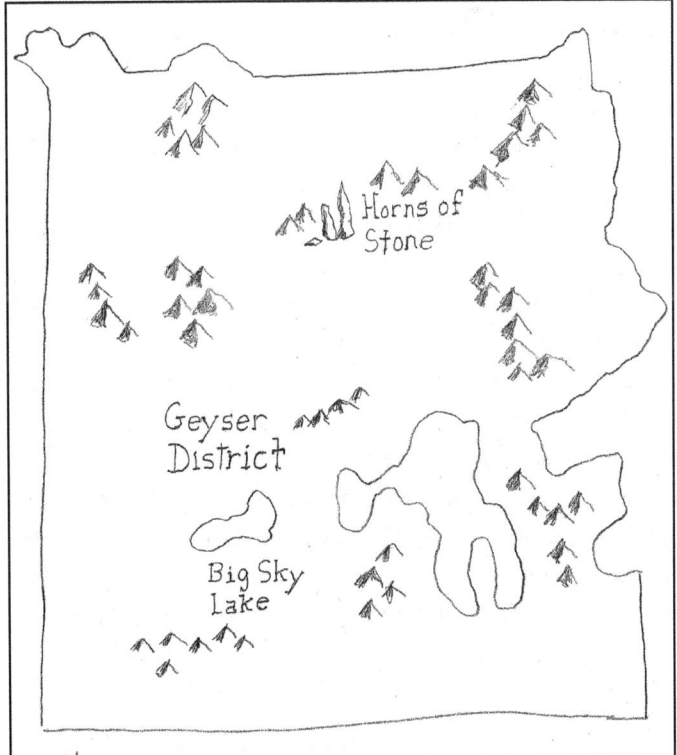

Since all of the messages, in and out, went through me I was beginning to get a picture of how widespread the damage was. The fire was now engulfing three districts; at least twenty percent of Lake, Potholes, and Geyser districts were burning or already blackened. The weather forecast called for more wind towards evening, and we had not had rainfall for three weeks, except for that light drizzle the day of our committee meeting, so the prospect for a quick end to the fire was not good. Zornova worked swiftly and efficiently directing the evacuation of the dead and wounded; she provided instructions for fire fighting parties, and calmly provided leaders for those who must flee or be consumed by the inferno. Even now gusts of wind spread ashes and set dust devils swirling across the clearing outside the station. Thirty-four thousand acres had already been consumed.

"Blinkers!" came through the intercom from Zornova's offices. "The fire may soon reach us. It is time for us to pack up and leave. I have sent for Cawdor to lead the office staff safely away from the blaze. Blinkers, you and I have another task, so we will not be traveling with the rest of the office staff."

"Yes, Zornova," I answered, knowing that this would undoubtedly involve more bison-back riding. I walked, as calmly as I could, from my office down the hall past other offices; I stopped at each office to ask all office staffers to assemble on the front porch. Once they were assembled, I announced that it was time to leave and that Cawdor would lead them to safety.

Soon Thimblewicket, Rittiticket, Pudge, and others were moving quickly along the narrow trail leading westward towards Trout Lake. Cawdor flew above the fleeing office workers, cawing as he went to assure them that the way was clear. Zornova is such a good leader, she had remained calm and in control in spite of this horrendous calamity. There had been minimal panic because Zornova's quiet strength gave everyone confidence and hope.

Flames were now visible atop Marmot Ridge; they would soon engulf the ranger station here in Prairie Dog Vale. I was just about to fetch Zornova when she emerged through the doors.

"Look Zornova," I wailed, "the fire has reached the ridge top and it will soon be upon us."

Zornova ignored my fear. "Get back aboard, Blinkers," she said calmly "I still need your help. Skeezer, Rutorina, and the other skunks in Dozema's skaggle are traditionalists, so in spite of the fire they are stubbornly following their practice of silently mourning the deceased for two days. They are in immediate danger, and we are the only ones available to rescue them.

I clamored up onto Zornova's shaggy back. Skunks! Wouldn't you just know they would pull something like this. Well, everyone knows that skunks are loyal and that they honor their dead by standing silently mourning the deceased for two days. They must also fast for these two days. Oh what shall we do I wondered, as we bounced towards Willow Meadow. I could not keep my eyes closed all the time now, for the smoke made me cough and sputter. We made it through Broken Fir Gap just ahead of the fire. Oh my goodness, we were heading directly towards the fire.

"Oh Zornova," I whined. "How shall we ever survive? You can't just expect to trot through the fire unharmed."

"Be calm, Blinkers," she answered, "we will drop downhill soon and follow Stonecrop Creek through the fire. But we must be quick, and we must hold our breaths through the worst of it. So be ready. And you must let me know if my fur catches on fire."

Almost before I could catch my breath, Zornova turned and rushed down the steep slope towards Stonecrop Creek, jumping over fallen trees, swerving and weaving between trees and boulders. I felt some sympathy now for rodeo cowboys as I hung on tightly. Then Zornova shouted "Now!" I gulped in a lungful of air and held my breath. Soon my lungs felt like they would burst and my heart pounded vigorously as Zornova clattered over the rocks of Stonecrop Creek. Zornova stumbled and lurched forward, so I went flying over her neck and horns into the creek. Just as I struggled up onto her back a burning tree crashed into the stream-bed behind us, narrowly missing Zornova's hind end. Steam and crackling engulfed us. But Zornova undeterred slogged forward through the shallows of Stonecrop Creek. Both of us were cough-ing and sputtering as we breathed in the smoke-filled air.

Fortunately, we soon passed from the smoke and flames into the smoldering forest beyond, left charred and black from the fire. Zornova continued following the creek; although it was slow going we could avoid the worst of the smoke. Silence surrounded us. No bird song, no skittering of small feet through the leaves and litter interrupted the quiet. Only rock and barren tree trunks remained to guard our passage. Suddenly the silence was interrupted as a tree crashed down to our right as the roots gave way. After what seemed like an endless ride through the blackened forest, we left Stonecrop Creek, climbed up over Fir Cone Ridge, and headed down again into Willow Meadow. The flames had skipped the meadow, which remained green and normal. But at any moment smoldering embers might be dropped by the wind and the whole meadow could flare up and burn quickly. Skeezer, Rutorina, and seven other skunks could be seen on the far side of the meadow. As we drew closer we could hear their whistle-like chant.

"Skeezer!" shouted Zornova, as we approached the skaggle of skunks.

"Yes, Zornova, what is it," answered Skeezer, obviously an-noyed at the interruption of their sacred funeral rite.

"You must all come at once or there will be nine more skunk funerals to attend. A huge fire is burning out of control, and you must all leave. You have been fortunate so far, as Willow Meadow has been spared, but that could change any moment," said Zornova, with both authority and control.

As Zornova spoke flames could be seen atop Fir Cone Ridge. The wind had shifted again and would drive the flames towards us. Smoke was already billowing towards us across the open meadow.

"Oh, all right Zornova, but which way should we go?" answered Skeezer. Perhaps the approaching flames and billowing smoke had been more convincing than Zornova's words.

Before Zornova could speak Menki, the eagle, swooped down and landed on a nearby stump.

"Zornova, there is no time to explain, you must travel up over Spiny Ridge, then go down across the highway," said Menki, who was almost out of breath.

I hopped down from Zornova's back. "You don't need to carry me now," I said, "I can easily keep up with the skunks."

Zornova took the lead while I brought up the rear. As you can imagine, it was hard to keep nine skunks moving. Even though we were in great danger from the fire they could not resist hesitating to overturn rocks and fallen branches in search of nuts, pinecones, and other edibles. Soon we were all out of breath from the climb. We looked back only to see that the fire had consumed most of Willow Meadow and would soon reach the base of the ridge we had just ascended. After a short minute's rest we scrabbled quickly down the other side. Soon we reached a faint trail, which allowed us to quicken our pace. But Spritzer, the youngest skunk, and Skeezer, the oldest, were beginning to tire.

"Zornova," I cried from the rear of our procession, "Skeezer and Spritzer are tiring rapidly. Could you give them a ride?"

Zornova retraced her steps towards us and then knelt down as the two ungainly skunks scrabbled up onto her back. All of us were now able to quicken our pace. The underbrush became thicker and thicker as we descended the far side of Spiny Ridge. Zornova charged through the underbrush helping to clear the path as we struggled through the tangle of shrubby plants and vines. I could not help but notice that she was bleeding in several places from wounds made by sharp limbs that had pierced her fur and skin. We kept on at this faster pace for what seemed like hours. Then suddenly Zornova halted. It was a moment before we could all catch our breath. Soon Zornova turned toward us and whispered,

"Skeezer and Spritzer you must climb down from my back immediately. There are firefighters coming through the trees towards us. We will find a gap between them, but they still may see us, so we must look as we are expected to look. Just over the next small rise is the highway, so no more talking until we cross the highway and are out of earshot of the humans."

Skeezer and Spritzer dismounted as best they could. Again we headed on through the underbrush. Below us and to our right a squad of firefighters was starting a backfire in an attempt to contain the blaze before it reached the highway. I think two of them may have seen us, so it was good that Skeezer and Spritzer were not bison-back riding. That might have seemed a bit odd, even under the present dire circumstances. People just never give us any credit for our intelligence. We moved on down and over the small rise before Zornova stopped us several hundred yards from the highway.

"Blinkers, you go ahead and find us a good place to cross the highway, someplace where there are no fire trucks or cars," whispered Zornova.

So down I went following a small streamlet that dribbled merrily down the rocky, brush covered slope. The sounds I heard as I approached the highway did not bode well. As soon as I was close enough I climbed a tree, only to discover a major traffic jam on the highway that stretched out below me. Cars, campers, and vans were bumper-to-bumper, moving southward very slowly. This was not good. How could our tired group of skunks make it across this crowded highway? I looked both south and north trying to find some alternative route. Then I recognized the bridge crossing over the south fork of Spiny Creek, about three hundred yards to the north. That bridge was high enough that even Zornova could fit beneath it. Quickly but carefully I climbed back down from my evergreen perch before I rushed back up the hill to report to Zornova.

"So you see," I said, breathing rapidly "we must go north, and then go under the bridge that crosses the south fork of Spiny Creek. Even you can fit beneath that bridge, and Skeezer, Spritzer, Rutorina, and the others can avoid the highway, which is just packed with tourists in their vans, campers, and cars."

"Good thinking, Blinkers," interrupted Zornova "let's get going. I will feel much better once we are on the other side of the highway."

Soon we were making our way beneath the bridge. Zornova had only a couple of inches clearance, but was able to pick her way along the creek as it flowed under the bridge. The honking cars and the sirens made the skunks nervous. They had to be soothed so they wouldn't raise their tails and spray in response to their fear. Once we reached the edge of the forest beyond the highway we climbed up out of the creek bed. The skunks became calmer, but Skeezer began to complain that his legs ached and Spritzer whined and complained that his paws hurt. The rest of the skunks looked a bit bedraggled as well. It was then that Zornova announced that she knew of a safe haven for us.

"We are not far from Big Sky Lake. Skeezer and Spritzer, you may climb up on my back again. We must hurry on to Beaver Island; there is no time to waste."

Wearily Skeezer and Spritzer ascended the slope of Zornova's back. Some of the other skunks grumbled, mumbling that they were tired too. But they all hurried on as best they could as the smoke moved across the sky to block out the sun. It was another two miles to Big Sky Lake, and then another half mile beyond that to Beaver Island. I made a mental note to cross skunk herding off my list of possible career alternatives.

Beaver Island

WHEN WE reached the lakeshore, Zornova stopped and crouched down so that Spritzer, and Skeezer could dismount. Then she said, "We can rest when we reach the island. Right now all of you must forage and fill your stomachs for there will not be much to eat on Beaver Island."

Nobody argued, for it had been a long and difficult day with no time for eating. The skunks set about devouring seedpods and berries while Zornova cropped the tall grass near the water's edge. I dug up some edible tubers and waded out into the lake to wash them. One by one, as each belly was filled the skunks returned to the water's edge and rested. Spritzer, the least accomplished forager, was the last to return.

As Spritzer ambled back towards our small group of refugees, Zornova spoke again "I can take five of you at a time. Blinkers you stay here with the four that remain.

It was almost a hundred yards from the shore to Beaver Island. Most of the distance was shallow water. The skunks had to be coaxed up onto Zornova's back, for they all feared the lake that seemed deep to them, even the shallow part that they would ford. Zornova waded slowly into the dark waters and then worked her way carefully between boulders and sunken logs. About two thirds of the way across, there was a shrill squeal from Skeezer; he became unsettled as Zornova began to swim through water too deep for wading. Soon they were on the island and Zornova struggled up out of the lake and unloaded her passengers.

Zornova returned quickly to collect the remaining skunks for her second trip to the island. Rutorina had to be awakened before she could climb aboard.

"Blinkers you climb on up too," Zornova said, "there's enough room on my back for you as well."

Though I could swim across, I was glad for a bison-back ride right now, for I was simply exhausted. It seemed like several days, rather than just part of one day, since we left the Geyser District Ranger Station to rescue this skaggle of nine very stubborn but timid skunks.

Zornova was approaching the deeper water, where she would need to swim, when she stumbled over an unseen log hidden within the darkness of the lake. Rutorina tumbled into the water squeaking madly. Without thinking I jumped in after her.

"You go on Zornova," I cried from the water, "I can bring Rutorina by myself."

Soon I regretted my confidence, for Rutorina, even though she was exhausted, thrashed and struggled so that I thought I would never get hold of her. Finally she began to tire and sink. I grabbed the thick fur of her neck with my jaws just before her nose sank below the surface. Rutorina, now totally wearied, was more cooperative. Even though my heart was pounding rapidly and my forelegs ached from paddling towards the shore, we soon reached the shallows surrounding Beaver Island. Rutorina, once released from my jaws, shambled ashore rapidly. Once ashore she climbed up onto a flat rock ledge and shook herself until she was no longer waterlogged.

"Oh, thank you Blinkers!" she gushed, as she gave me a skunk-stinky kiss on my cheek.

"Just think nothing of it, Rutorina," I answered, "it's all in the line of duty you know. It's nothing to get worked up about. You go on now and find a comfortable place to rest."

Zornova limped over to the shore. She had cut her right fore-leg badly and there was a steady flow of blood from several nasty looking wounds.

"Thank you, Blinkers," she said wearily. "You have been a great help to me today."

"Oh Zornova," I responded, "you have saved the day for us! Without your resolve and calm head none of us would have made it this far. We are now safe at least. You stay here while I look for some lichen and spiders' webs to staunch your wound. You need to rest more than any of us; you are the one who has worked so hard to get us to this haven of safety."

I hurried off to hunt for medicinal herbs and other first aid materials among the large boulders on the island. It is called Beaver Island, because the southwest end has two white and gleaming tooth-shaped boulders. Moving from the boulders towards the northeast the island widens outward, forming a shape similar to a beaver's body; then, both sides taper inward towards what would be the base of the beaver's tail. From there, a flat and treeless tail-shaped extension stretches out into the lake. We had come ashore near the base of the tail. Soon I found the lichen and spiders' webs I needed and headed back towards Zornova. Once the lichen and spiders' webs were applied the bleeding slowed and then stopped completely. Fortunately, I had been able to find several herbs that would ease the pain caused by Zornova's wounds. I remember her chewing them slowly, but I do not know what happened next, for exhaustion overcame me and I slept.

Flapping wings awakened me from sleep. It must have been morning, but the dawn, smoke-filled and murky, was difficult to differentiate from night. Gondzor circled as he slowed to land. Almost as soon as he touched down on the flat rocky surface he and Zornova were in a deep discussion about what faced us all. It was clear from their gestures and their facial expressions that they were both deeply concerned about the district and all who lived there. As they discussed the situation Zornova and Gondzor had walked out part way onto the treeless tail of Beaver Island. Gondzor did most of the talking. Zornova listened intently, nodding her head occasionally to acknowledge important facets of Gondzor's report.

Soon Gondzor motioned for me to come to them. Oh how my legs ached, and how hungry I was.

"Blinkers," said Zornova, "the situation is not good. I cannot stay here any longer, for there are many who are in danger and many more who will soon need food and medical attention. You are to stay here until you are sent for. Gondzor tells me that the fire has not yet crossed the highway. It will soon be under control in this sector, but in the southwest part of Geyser District it is still burning out of control. I must go there immediately. Gondzor will help direct me from above. Assemble the skaggle of skunks for me and I will tell them what they need to know before I leave."

"Yes Zornova," I answered, before walking back stiffly, because my legs still ached, to find the skunks resting under some trees not far from the base of the tail.

"Come along all of you," I announced, "Zornova must go now and she wishes to speak with you before she leaves."

Moaning softly they padded out onto the beaver's tail where Zornova and Gondzor awaited them. They arranged themselves according to rank and authority, and then waited quietly for Zornova to begin.

"All of you have been very brave," she began. "You have followed my instructions and persevered under pressure. I must go now to take care of the many other refugees and those who have been injured. Blinkers will stay with you. If you have any needs Blinker's will do his best to help you. I will send you information as often as I have couriers available. Though you are weary you must keep up hope. Farewell for now."

Skeezer, since he was the eldest skunk present, replied. "All of us thank you for rescuing us. We would certainly be dead by now if you and Blinkers had not come to save us. We know that you are responsible for all who live in the Geyser District, so we do not need to detain you here. You have brought us to a safe haven, and for that we all thank you."

Soon after Zornova and Gondzor left the island together I turned toward the skunks, all of whom looked a little dazed from their ordeal, and said, "You must all conserve energy and ration the food that is available on this small island. We may well be here for several days. You must not give in to worry, for Zornova and Gondzor will not abandon us. Skeezer, you shall be responsible for the rationing of food. Rutorina, you will keep lookout from the Beaver's teeth, and warn us if the fire turns this way again. Everyone else should rest and stay quiet to conserve your energy."

After so much hurrying on the previous day, time slackened its pace to a crawl. Smoke turned the usually bright reflections from the lake's surface into a sooty, ominous looking brew. Ash filtered in on the wind and breathing became an effort interrupted by coughing. At first Spraybreath and Spritzer set about grooming themselves, plucking burrs and spiders' webs from their fur. But they were soon discouraged because ash began to drift down upon them, recoating them with new layers of ash before they could remove the old layers of grime. Their inability to clean themselves left them despondent. Even though we were presently in little danger, we felt weighed down by the calamity and uncertainty.

On the day Zornova departed little happened. We spent our time resting and sleeping awakened only by fits of smoke-induced coughing. Skeezer oversaw the rationing of food for the skunks. Late in the afternoon, though it was difficult to be sure, with so little sun filtering through the smoke and ash, I waded into the shallows to wash my food. The water's surface was gritty with ash and several small fish floated belly up. I could not get my food as clean as I liked. All of us were depressed in spirit and afraid of the news we might receive, about friends and family members hurt or killed by the flames. As I waded back towards the shore, I heard squealing and hissing coming from the island.

"No more food for you, Spraybreath," shouted Skeezer.

"Get out of my way, you old geezer Skeezer," Spraybreath yelled back.

"You little squirt you, I'll teach you to sass me," Skeezer bellowed back defiantly.

I hurried ashore to put an end to this dispute. Wouldn't you know it, as soon as I take a break for lunch, some ruckus had to erupt.

"Skeezer, could you please tell me the cause of this dispute? This is not the time for arguing, or for snarling insults at one another; we must take care of each other," I said as I approached the pair of sparring skunks.

"Just buzz off masked secretary," snarled Spraybreath, before she turned to hiss and snarl at Skeezer.

"Well my goodness you are a rude one," I replied, for I was determined not to let anger intrude. "Go ahead Skeezer, you give me your story, and then Spraybreath you can give me your version."

"Thank you, Blinkers," replied Skeezer with authority. "This little stink-tailed piglet is eating too much. This is the second time today she has gone foraging without my permission."

"We can do without the name-calling, Skeezer," I replied calmly. "Now Spraybreath, what have you to say?"

"Well old Skeezer keeps telling me what to do," whined Spraybreath, no longer quite so defiant. "I'm hungry. I'm a growing skunk and I need to eat regularly."

"Yes we understand Spraybreath, all of us are hungry," I explained. "But we must ration our food so that we don't starve and die. Now I want you Spraybreath to apologize to Skeezer, and then I want you Skeezer to apologize to Spraybreath. And I don't want to hear any more name-calling. And Spraybreath, I want you to do as Skeezer says."

After their mutual apologies the skunks calmed down and waddled back to the base of the beaver's tail. Grubsy was on watch, but would soon return when Crooked Stripe took over as lookout. Just as Grubsy could be heard wheezing as he returned from watch duty, two large forms emerged from the deep water. From the silhouettes I could tell that two moose were approaching. Neither had antlers so they were both females. One was smaller and younger.

As they approached I called out to them, "Who are you?"

"Oh don't be such a busybody Blinkers," came back across the water. My heart sank, for it was Tromengard and Udena. I did not really want to deal with the contentious Tromengard, but I must be civil. As a public servant one learns to hold his tongue. One learns not to say just what one might like.

"Welcome, Udena and Tromengard," I called back. Both of them had stopped chewing on the plants they had plucked from beneath the water's surface. "What brings you here?"

Tromengard answered back, with her nose high in the air, "Just what business is it of yours to ask about our comings and goings?"

I did not reply, for such insolence did not deserve a reply. I waited, knowing that Tromengard liked to talk; I knew that she could not resist her desire to be the center of attention.

It was not long before Tromengard spoke again, this time with less ostentation. "The wind has shifted and the fire has crossed the highway and is heading this way. It will not be long before the fire reaches the shore of Big Sky Lake. So we have come to Beaver Island for refuge. We did not expect to find anyone here."

"We were hoping that the fire would not come this way. You are welcome to join us here," I answered "Zornova has left me in charge here before taking her leave. We arrived yesterday afternoon after fleeing from Willow Meadow."

Tromengard moved closer to the shore then she stopped and started backing up again. "Oh gracious," she cried, "You are here with a skaggle of little stinkers aren't you? Well, you must all leave. You know that Udena is so sensitive. Surely you must know about her allergies. There is no other way; you must leave so that we can stay here safely. Get along now, all of you!"

"That is enough silliness from you, Tromengard. You may stay or you may leave, but none of us are leaving this island until Zornova sends us instructions," I answered. The nerve of that pompous moose!

"Look, Blinkers," shouted Spraybreath. "The fire is coming." We looked westward and saw that the sky was glowing brighter.

"Listen, all of you, and that includes you Tromengard—for I am in charge here until orders to the contrary arrive from Zornova," I shouted. "When the fire gets closer we must all stay low to avoid the smoke. We will stay on the far side of the island. Tromengard and Udena, you are to stay in the water so that you will be breathing near the surface. I will keep watch to make sure that no sparks ignite and burn our refuge. If a fire should start on the island all of you must help put it out."

The skunks shambled around to the east side of the island. Tromengard and Udena continued to browse in the shallow water surrounding the island while I climbed to the top of a grassy mound near the center of the beaver's back, to watch for sparks and flames. Within half an hour flames reached the shoreline across the shallows from the island. I left my post on the grassy mound, for the smoke had become too thick, making breathing difficult. Though I could hear chewing sounds offshore, Tromengard and Udena could not be seen through the smoke that hung thickly in the air surrounding the island, which was lost in the darkness that felt like eternal night. I began to patrol the island and found the skunks huddled beneath a small rocky ledge. They were clearly agitated by the nearness of danger, so Skeezer told stories of skunk bravery to keep them calm and to encourage them.

I stopped briefly to listen. Skeezer was reciting the legend of Scampers the Brave, a skunk that had lived long ago. "Scampers was not a big strong skunk like Stomper the Great, the wise leader of the skunks who had traveled westward across the arid land to reach the park. No, Scampers was a bit on the puny side, but that did not keep him from acting bravely when bravery was what was needed. Scampers lived sixteen generations past, before the time of airplanes, before roads were hard and black, before our ancestors catered to the needs of tourists with their silly antics. Scampers had saved several skaggles of skunks who were trapped on what had become an island, much like Beaver Island, in Eagle Lake several weeks journey from Big Sky Lake.

"It was during one of the great spring rains. Every day the sky was gray; it was as if all birds were crying at once. The rain caused the snow to melt and the waters to rise. This trapped the skunks that had been attending a yearly meeting at Meadow Point that extended out into Eagle Lake. None of the skunks had thought to check the low area between the point and the rest of the lakeshore, for they had been too concerned with the meeting and with keeping as warm and dry as possible. They were gathered in a grove of trees since that was the driest place they could find. But Scampers was famished and wandered off looking for pinecone seeds. His hunger led him back along the trail they had all followed to the point. He wasn't paying too much attention until the trail ended abruptly in the lake.

"At first Scampers thought he might have taken a wrong turn, but that was not the case for he could see the trail winding up from the other side of the water. Scampers ran back and told the twenty-nine skunks gathered beneath the trees that they might very well be in some danger. However, for the next several days everything would be okay, for the skunks had sufficient food and shelter under the trees.

"But each day Scampers went to where the trail ended in the water. And each day the distance got shorter and shorter as the water of Eagle Lake kept rising. Soon, there would not be much left of Meadow Point, and then what would they do? Scampers could get none of the other skunks to think about this issue. Stinker, Wide Stripe, and the other skunks were too busy arguing about food gathering rights agreements that involved these three skunk skaggles. So Scampers decided he would have to find a solution. He spent many hours at the trail's end concentrating on a solution to this dilemma that the other skunks were heedlessly ignoring. As he sat there he began to notice several trees that stuck up from the flood. He noticed, as he stared into the wet gray atmosphere that some of the trees had begun to tilt. He waded out into the water to the nearest tilting tree. He discovered that the rock and soil around the roots had washed away weakening the tree roots hold, causing it to tilt. Scampers returned to the shore to think about this. He waded back out and began to dig away at the rock and stone. After working for hours the tree began to tilt some more. Scampers had dug only on one side of the tree with the hope that it would tilt and fall in a particular direction. He dug some more until he was totally wearied. As he watched from the shore, the tree shuddered as the roots gave way and fell across the water towards the mainland.

"Scampers raced back to the other skunks, but they were still verbally wrangling. After a moment's thought he gathered several young skunks, Black Hips, White Ears, and Stinknose, and said, 'Are you guys as bored as I am?' Of course they all answered 'we were about to turn to stone.' Scampers told them he had found a great way to have some fun while all the old ones wore out their brains with worthless talking. These three young skunks were so bored they would have found a snail race exciting. Anyway, they followed Scampers back to the fallen tree readily enough. After a couple hours of concerted effort they felled several more trees in the waterlogged group.

"By the end of the day Scampers and his pals had made a tree bridge to the mainland. It wasn't pretty, but it was functional. The next problem was how to get the rest of the skunks to shut up long enough to recognize the danger they were in. By nightfall, there might not be much left of Meadow Point if the floodwaters continued to rise. Scampers soon had a plan. 'I need a volunteer to fake a drowning; which one of you is willing to be a hero?' Nobody wanted to be a hero. So Scampers would have to fake his own drowning and depend upon his pals to make a loud enough ruckus to draw their elders to the shore. Once the plan was set Scampers crossed partway over the tree bridge to a shallow spot.

He jumped into the water signaling for the other three to race back to the council area and scream and carry on.

"Well, the scheme worked. Black Hips, White Ears, and Stinknose raced into the council area beneath the trees acting like crazed maniacs. After about five minutes the elder skunks had got the message that Scampers was drowning in the floodwaters. 'Floodwaters?' asked Stinker, like the thickheaded lummox he was. Anyway, every member of the three skaggles rushed to the shore; it was a very brief rush since the water had continued to rise. Scampers did his part almost too well; he screamed then thrashed about until all of the skunks raced out onto the tree bridge led by White Ears and Stinknose. Black Hips encouraged the remaining slackers onto the bridge.

"As his rescuers neared, Scampers scampered up onto the logs and toward the mainland after calling Stinker a cow-brained numbskull. This horrid insult caused Stinker and the others to follow in hot pursuit, and just in time, for upstream a logjam broke sending a grand wall of water into the lake. Just as the last of the skunks jumped from the log bridge to the shore, a large wave washed over the log bridge. The floodwaters continued to rise until all of Meadow Point was submerged. Even Stinker forgave Scampers his insult. Ever since the rescue Scampers has been remembered for both his ingenuity and bravery.

After the story ended I continued my patrol. Tromengard and Udena could not be seen through the smoke that hung thickly in the air surrounding the island, which was lost in the darkness that felt like night.

On another one of my patrols around the island I was able to discern the heads of Tromengard and Udena silhouetted against the flames still raging just beyond the lakeshore. The wind began to pick up with the coming of morning, and I worried that burning debris might drift across the lake onto the island and set fires that would burn us out and leave us a barren refuge. It was just then that I noticed a grass fire up ahead. I rushed forward towards the patch of fiercely burning grass.

"Tromengard! Udena! Come her at once!" I shouted. Then I jumped into the water to protect my fur from fire. As soon as I emerged from the water I snatched up fir boughs, dipped them into the lake and then began beating at the flames. Tromengard approached dripping with water with Udena close behind. Both moose pawed at the fire while dripping water from their shaggy bodies. Back and forth, in and out of the lake they went, until the fire was doused and beaten back to ashes. A blackened patch of ground about twenty-five by thirty feet in dimension gave evidence to the danger we had all faced. All three of us washed the soot from our fur as best we could in the murky ash laden waters surrounding Beaver Island.

By the time the fire was out the flames along the opposite shore had subsided, leaving smoldering brush and trees behind. I hurried back along the island's eastern shore to check on the skunks. They were still cowering under the overhang where I had left them.

"You can breathe easier," I told them "for the fire is now dying down on the mainland. We had a small brush fire on the island, but that too has been extinguished."

Some sunlight managed to filter through the smoke. Our small green island looked rather isolated against the blackened backdrop of the lakeshore in the distance.

"If there is still food available, then you should go ahead and eat," I said tiredly.

Skeezer, Spraybreath, Spritzer, Rutorina, and Grubsy wandered about forlornly hunting for something to eat. I headed into the water to wash the bit of food I had found. After stretching out my few bites to create the illusion that I had dined at length and eaten a great deal, I took a nap, after placing Skeezer in charge.

I was awakened by the shrill voice of Rutorina. "Get up, get up Blinkers! Menki is here with a message from Zornova."

I hastened to the base of the Beaver's tail where Menki was preening her feathers. No doubt she was trying, perhaps futilely, to remove some of the soot and ash.

"It's good to see you Menki," a said sleepily. "What message has Zornova sent?"

Menki answered wearily, for she had been kept busy carrying messages all over the district and beyond. "The news is not good, Blinkers. The fire has charred seventy-five percent of the Geyser District; it's the worst fire in anyone's memory. Other neighboring districts are almost as badly burnt. At least the fire is now under control and should be out soon, unless the winds rise again. Many are now homeless and there is a shortage of food and good drinking water. Some animals have been tempted to eat flesh. But there is also good news, Ranger Gormla of the Spruce District has invited our refugees to recuperate there until we can begin to sort through the mess in our own district."

"I'm glad to hear at least some good news," I replied. "Some are really eating flesh?"

"Sadly, yes," groaned Menki.

The eating of flesh was strictly taboo in all of the park's districts. We knew that animals outside of the park ate flesh. We knew that the stronger animals caught and killed the weaker animals; we knew it was common for cougars and bears to eat prairie dogs, deer, and rabbits. Beyond the boundaries of our pristine park, we knew that raccoons ate crawfish, and otters ate fish, and birds ate insects. But within the park we believed that the creator did not intend for us to kill others so that we might live. So we ate only those foods that came from plants. We ate berries and seeds; some of us also ate tree bark or tubers. Killing was an evil that would lead to the destruction of the peace that allowed us to live in harmony with all other animals—all mammals, all birds, all fish, all amphibians, and all reptiles.

I put an end to my cogitations about animals killing animals and focused again on Menki and what she had come to tell us. "How are Zornova and Gondzor holding up?" I asked.

"They are tired, but well; all of us are tired," Menki answered. "That reminds me, Zornova said that the bison Tennial would come tomorrow or the following day to help all of you get back to the mainland, and then on to Spruce District, to the south."

Spruce District

TENNIAL DID come and we made our way slowly through the charred landscape, avoiding hot spots and flare-ups. It was a long and dirty trip. All of us were disheartened by the destruction and devastation the fire had wrought upon the mountains, streams, and valleys we called home. But now we are here in Shooting Star Meadow, surrounded by green trees, green grass, and with the cool and clean waters of Shooting Star Creek flowing nearby. Thousands of animals from Geyser District are camped in the meadow and adjacent forest. Other refugees are on the other side of Grey Jay Ridge, to the southwest, in Marmot Meadow. To the northeast we can see the dead and silent trees of Grizzly Ridge; they remind us of why we are all gathered here.

Zornova was, as I expected, tired from attending to the multitude of problems we faced, but I am glad to be back where I can be useful to her again. Tonight we will have a general meeting of all of us gathered here; we will discuss what we shall do next. We hope that we will have some more information, so we will be able to determine when we can move back to our homes in Geyser District. Gondzor, Cawdor, Jet, Menki, and others should be back with their scouting reports in time for the meeting. For now, I am taking a census to determine how many Geyser District residents are here in Shooting Star Meadow. I was engaged in putting my list in alphabetical order when up pranced Pabatackle.

"So you are a certified hero now, are you?" he taunted. "You have saved a whole skaggle of stink bottles and two moosies, yes?"

"I helped, that's true," I answered curtly, not wanting to be distracted by Pabatackle's prattling diversion.

"And just what is the ever-busy district secretary doing now, may I ask?" he continued, "are you planning a speech for tonight's meeting? Are you going to receive the stink bottle retrieval medal of honor? Why were you so brave, what difference would it make if there were fewer stink bottles?"

"Look Pabatackle, I have important work to do," I replied "why don't you go look for berries or something, or go for a nice swim?"

"Maybe I will do just that old foody-wash fingers," he answered before turning to prance away.

The meeting was set for five in the afternoon. By four-thirty most of the animals were assembled just below Gray Rock Point. Cawdor had already returned and was speaking with Zornova. Menki was circling above, preparing to land. Below, in the meadow, groups of animals speculated about what would happen next. Hope was intermixed with fear, for all who were gathered here were refugees. All of the certainties of daily life had been replaced by doubts and fears, many of which were left unspoken.

At a quarter to five Gondzor came gliding down to Gray Rock Point, where Zornova awaited him. Gondzor could be seen gesticulating with his wings and speaking quickly, as he reported to Zornova.

At five o'clock silence spread across Shooting Star Meadow and Zornova turned towards the expectant crowd. She began with a summary of the reports from the scouting sorties to all parts of Geyser District. "The good news is that the fire is out. The bad news is that most of our district is now a burnt-out ruin. The district headquarters building burned to the ground; many nests, burrows, dens, and other living quarters have been badly damaged or destroyed. The toll on insect life has been especially high. But many others, especially the newborn young, were killed or badly burned by the flames. Yet we should be thankful that most of us have escaped, and that this fire came in late spring rather than late fall for green shoots will soon rise up from the ashes and begin to rejuvenate our meadows and forests. Now we must decide, as a group, what to do next.

Morgorgor spoke up with her slow, authoritative voice, "Madame Ranger, should we not appoint a committee to oversee our return to our homeland? Shouldn't we also send agents to consult with the refugees from other districts to ascertain what they plan to do? And, in addition, shouldn't there be a park-wide committee to coordinate and guide us so that we may work smoothly together?"

Wanda, who had to shout to be heard, yelled, "I second Morgorgor's motion."

In the voting that followed all of Morgorgor's proposals were approved by those gathered in the meadow. Representatives of other Geyser District refugees, camped at various and scattered places, also voted for these proposals. After the voting concluded a hubbub arose as various animals called out the names of those they wanted on the proposed committee.

"It is time for silence now," Zornova intoned. "I thank you for all of your good suggestions for committee members. A list of those appointed to this committee will be posted by tomorrow noon. Tonight the District Council will meet to select individuals to serve on the new resettlement committee."

Just then, Tromengard spoke up. "The perpetrator of this fire must be punished. We must know who started the fire and then see that the guilty party or parties are punished. As you know my daughter Udena is so sensitive to smoke, with her allergies and all; well, this fire has been a dreadful stress for my daughter. I want retribution!"

"Here-here, find the guilty ones," was shouted by many voices. "Yes! Yes! Punish the guilty ones!"

"Our lands are destroyed, we have no place to live, string up the guilty ones!" shouted other angry voices.

Oh my, oh my, what a ruckus, what a fuss! I thought. Surely nobody would have set such a fire on purpose. What will Zornova do now?

"Quiet please," interjected Zornova, with volume and authority. "The District Council has already begun an investigation into the cause of the fire. We will continue to do so. However, for now, our top priority is to see to the needs of all of us who are here, and in Marmot Meadow, and scattered elsewhere. Our main goal is to rebuild what has been lost; we need no retribution, and vengeance will not bring back one shred of the peace we have lost. I will not tolerate any more spiteful talk, for it will only add to our misery and do nothing to help us solve the many difficulties we face."

"I know," she continued "that many of you seek news of your friends and the kin who were separated from you in the confusion following the blaze. Gondzor has news for many of you about these sought-after family members and friends. He will let you know what he knows as soon as this meeting is over. Now, unless there is more business to attend to we will close the meeting. We will meet here again the day after tomorrow."

No one spoke up, so numerous animals wanting to know about their family members, neighbors, and friends, soon accosted Gondzor.

"Is there any news of my cousin Ethelsnappit," cried out Thimblewicket.

Quickett, the tree frog, chirruped, from his perch atop Keeble's head, "Gondzor, has anyone seen my wife Jumpup? I couldn't find her when we were told to evacuate our homes."

"If you will just line up here behind Thimblewicket I can answer your questions," Gondzor calmly assured everyone. "No need to push and shove."

I escaped that hubbub and followed Zornova back to our temporary district headquarters. I had made a large hollow log into a temporary office for myself. Thimblewicket had adapted a hollowed out stump to meet her needs as dispatcher. Zornova worked from beneath a large fir tree close by. We were making do with what we had. I certainly wished that I had my computer again, but no doubt it was melted into uselessness by now. Paper and pencil would have to do for the present, and even that was hard to come by these days.

After reaching my temporary quarters in the hollow log, I transferred the shorthand minutes of our recent meeting into longhand. Oh there was so much to do. Today I had taken a census of Shooting Star Meadow, and tomorrow I would be heading to Marmot Meadow to accomplish the same task there. As soon as Gondzor was available I must find out from him any information on refugees and missing animals. At last count there were 8,350 mammals, 12,873 birds, 97,398 insects (but only those we keep records of), 3,984 fish, and 1,843 reptiles, 23,462 amphibians. Oh what a dither and mess. Here in Shooting Star Meadow there were twelve grizzly bears, seventeen black bears, twenty-two moose, fifteen elk, forty-three mule deer, 193 golden mantled ground squirrels, etc., etc."

"Blinkers," Zornova repeated. "I need your help with my bandages; will you please attend to them now?"

"Oh my, yes, Zornova, most certainly," I answered. "I am so busy with the census that I didn't hear you right away. I am so sorry. How are your injuries? Are they healing well? How are things looking back in the district? Have you talked to Gondzor yet about what we must do next?"

"Blinkers, if you will give me a moment I can answer at least some of your questions," interrupted Zornova. "My cuts are healing just fine and the pain is almost gone. Things are still looking pretty black back in Geyser District. No, Gondzor has not yet spoken to me about what he knows, but he should be here soon to give me his full report."

I had removed the old bandages and was putting on new bandages when Gondzor settled wearily onto the ground in front of us. "I am just about finished, Zornova, then you and Gondzor can talk in private," I said.

"No Blinkers, you might as well stay," replied Zornova. "You might as well know what we are up against. Whenever you are ready Gondzor, you may begin."

Gondzor settled more comfortably into a pile of cedar boughs and then spoke, though it was clear that he was very tired. "There is good news and bad news. Almost all of the animals are accounted for and very few have not shown up somewhere. Almost all animals have been transported to refugee camps, and the others are in transit to camps. The infirmary at Marmot Meadow is full, but most of the injuries are not severe. The forecast is for several days of rain, so we may have some flooding, but at least the earth will be watered and new life will sprout forth. Many of our refugees are in good spirits, but many others are despairing. Some of the latter are lethargic and have no desire to continue on, especially those that lost their young. Rumors are flying through the camps. Some rumors are of plagues to come, others say that humans started the fires on purpose to burn us out, and still others say that some of us became so hungry that they ate flesh."

Here Gondzor stopped for a moment to rest. "Zornova, you are to attend a meeting of the district rangers," he continued. "It is scheduled for one week from today in Falls Meadow, near the park headquarters. You should have no trouble getting there in three days time."

"Yes, and by the time I need to leave we should have a better picture of what we face when we return to Geyser District," interjected Zornova. "Did White Skull call this meeting?"

"No Menthes, the assistant head ranger, called the meeting," answered Gondzor "White Skull died in the flames while attempting to rescue Throphop and Pink Ear's son Hoppit." It took Gondzor a moment to compose himself for he and White Skull the bald eagle had been good friends for many years. They had gone on many flying journeys together. Then Gondzor continued,

"Menthes wants to make sure that our resettlement plans are carefully coordinated. She asked that all district rangers be ready to give a full report, and be able to outline the most important needs of their districts."

"Well," said Zornova, "we will certainly be busy for the next several days. Blinkers, you will go to Marmot Meadow tomorrow, as planned. Gondzor, you must rest until tomorrow afternoon, and then you should visit the scattered parties of refugees to the north and east. I will visit those refugees gathered further west. In three days we will meet here to coordinate our reports, prior to our scheduled meeting."

"The report of flesh eating is troubling," Zornova murmured. "We know that animals outside the park eat the flesh of other animals. But here, in the haven of our parklands, this is only a rare occurrence. We know that killing is something that can be learned; we know that any of us is capable of killing. But most of us would find killing another animal, no matter how small, to be utterly abhorrent. Gondzor and Blinkers, we must find out if there is a connection between these killings and this state of lethargy that so many of our refugees are plagued with. Blinkers, when you go to Marmot Meadow find out what you can. Interview any animal known to have eaten flesh. Gondzor, as you travel the district pay attention to any possible connections between flesh eating and lethargy."

The three of us parted on this gloomy note. Flesh eating had seldom been an issue and all of us knew that it destroyed the true harmony of nature where it was practiced. Humans were the worst offenders, and just look at the messes they were constantly involved in. I ambled back to my temporary quarters in a bit of a mental fog.

I found myself standing next to my log headquarters inert. This would not do for it would be a busy day tomorrow, so I must get some sleep. But first I must gather my things. I will need pencils and paper and a small pack, and . . . oh I wish I had my calculator, but it is all burnt and ruined now. Soon, however, I had gathered together what I would need, so I went off to sleep in my hollow log, just north of Shooting Star Meadow.

Early the next morning I was startled awake by an intensely noxious smell. Once the sleep was rubbed from my eyes I could see a dark face and two glowing black eyes staring back at me. I was so befuddled by the odoriferous vision that I was startled out of my nightly repose. Seeing what I hoped was a dream phantom led me to jump up so quickly that I bumped my head on the roof of my temporary home in the hollow log. Almost at once small paws were stroking my head and small squeaky sounds preceded any speech.

"My poor, silly hero," tittered Rutorina.

"What can I do for you at this early hour," I responded, barely able to disguise my disgust at this unwanted interruption of my sleep.

"I am so sorry that I startled you. Please forgive me for my part in causing you injury," she simpered, in response. "But I spoke with Gondzor yesterday. And he gave me permission to accompany you on your trip today to Marmot Meadow."

Great, just what I needed, a moonstruck skunk who could barely remember how to find food, is supposed to help me with my count of refugees! "I guess that if Gondzor has authorized you to come with me, then you might as well come along. Here, you take the pack with emergency medicines and first aid supplies. My pack is full of registers and messages for family members who may be at Marmot Meadow."

Just as we were about to leave Shooting Star Meadow, up pranced Pabatackle.

"Greetings old fishy one and old stinky one! How are my little love mammals doing this fine morning? Have you both been having a smoochy-good time?" chirruped Pabatackle before rolling over in a heap of laughter.

Somewhat irritated by this disrespectful greeting I replied in a very serious and dignified manner: "Good morning mirthful one, what can I do for you. Be quick for we need to be on our way, we haven't time for silliness now."

Instead of replying seriously, that rascal of an otter smirked and said, "Going on a date, how wonderful! You are in luck for I have come to perform my community duty as chaperone."

"We aren't going for a date and we don't need a chaperone!" I responded tartly.

"Don't be silly, of course you do—a dapper raccoon and a perfumed skunk—you will no doubt elope if I do not keep you in sight at every moment. Actually, I have been assigned to go with you. Don't look so stiff and offended, for surely your trip to Marmot Meadow will be much less dull with me along."

"And just who was it that assigned you to this party?" I answered with as much dignity as I could muster.

"The goose himself, your pompousness!" replied Pabatackle.

"Okay, okay, if Gondzor says you are to come, then come along you must, but I don't want you getting in my way or causing any kind of trouble," I responded.

Don't worry your officiousness; I will leave the sleek and waddling Rutorina to you alone! And, as usual, I will be on my best behavior."

Yeah right, I thought as I set off to the southeast. Rutorina came shambling along behind me. Pabatackle gleefully frolicking back and forth and hither and thither brought up the rear of our sadly undisciplined party. Soon, however, we were climbing up the eastern end of Gray Jay Ridge. It was slow going for there were many tangles of blackened and fallen trees and tumbled stones to be avoided. We had to be careful not to kick up the ashes that blanketed the ground or a fit of coughing would soon follow. Pabatackle was, as you might guess, the first to complain.

"Why couldn't we follow the stream, instead of going overland through this nasty realm of ash?" whimpered Pabatackle.

"I'm so sorry if this hardship is inconvenient for you Pabatackle. I didn't ask you to come along. The stream would also make for slow and laborious travel because of landslides and fallen trees. Anyway, Rutorina and I needed to carry packs with important materials that would be ruined if they were to get wet!" I responded.

Fortunately the path was narrow so Rutorina could not walk alongside me very often. When the path was wide and unobstructed she would try to catch up. She kept staring at me, her face all google-eyed. At least she did that until she ran into a boulder while she was staring at me instead of paying attention to where she was going. After her run-in with the boulder a nasty bump arose on her head and she paid more attention to the path we followed.

Shortly before noon we reached the northern edge of Marmot Meadow. Much of the meadow and the forest to the south and east had escaped the worst of the fire. It was a relief to fill our eyes with green again after our travel through ashes and blackness and chaotic rubble.

Romla, who was in charge of the refugee camp at Marmot Meadow, bounded over to meet us a few moments after we entered the meadow.

"It is good to see you Blinkers, and I see you have brought two capable assistants with you," intoned Romla with her deep voice. "I have sent for Grip, a marmot and one of the inhabitants of this meadow, to assist you in making your account. Rutorina, could you take those medical supplies on over to the southwest edge of the meadow, and turn them over to Thicket, who is in charge of the infirmary. Pabatackle, your father and mother are camping out near the stream at the southeast end of the meadow." Both Rutorina and Pabatackle hesitated to follow their instructions.

"Go along you two, I need to give some messages to Romla, and she may have messages for me to take back with me." So Rutorina shambled off towards the infirmary as Pabatackle headed in the opposite direction to visit his parents.

"Thank you, Blinkers, for sending them along. I do have a message for you to take back to Zornova and Gondzor. Our infirmary is beginning to fill with animals that have no physical symptoms of distress. Yet these refugees are lethargic, refuse to eat and do little but sleep. Thicket is becoming quite worried by the numbers. She and Gimlet are working day and night to figure out what can be done to get her patients to eat and give them back their will to live. However, thus far neither has been able to figure out what will get them back on their feet. If something is not done soon the whole meadow will be one large infirmary, and soon after that a morgue."

"That is very troubling," I said, shocked at the seriousness of Romla's words. "I will gather data for the census as quickly as I can."

"Knowing that you would arrive, I asked Grip to organize each animal species in a particular area to make the counting easier. Grip has made lists of all of the individuals, by name, for each species, so you should be able to finish your work this afternoon," said Romla with some urgency in her voice. "I need Gondzor and Zornova both working to solve this problem of depression and despondency."

"This is most serious, most serious. Thank you for making my job here so much easier." As I finished speaking, a handsome Marmot scrambled up a slight rise towards us. "You must be Grip. I'm Blinkers; it's good to meet you. It sounds as though you've got things well in hand."

Grip replied crisply, "Good to meet you Blinkers. Everyone was organized, but that otter you brought along with you is raising a ruckus, trying to get a game of King of the Stream going. As a result of his disturbance things are not as neat as they once were. However, with the help of Swat, one of your district's grizzlies, the situation should soon be in good shape again. Come along with me. We will start with the birds over in that stand of trees just beyond that mound of boulders."

From gray jays, to woodpeckers, to flickers, to ground squirrels we went counting and tabulating. I collected a pack full of messages for relatives back in Shooting Star Meadow. By late afternoon, thanks to Grip's help, I was finished. Fortunately Romla had requested that both Pabatackle and Rutorina stay behind to entertain the refugees encamped in Marmot Meadow. Rutorina would sing and Pabatackle, who seemed able to lift the spirits of those despondent patients at the infirmary with his antics and mirth, were both to remain a day or two.

"Romla, getting Rutorina and Pabatackle out of the way was a stroke of genius. I thank you ever so much. Be sure that Gondzor and Zornova will get your report, and I shall certainly see that they understand just how serious the situation is. Well, I'd best be off while there is still plenty of light." I bid Romla and Grip adieu and headed back up over the east end of Gray Jay Ridge.

My journey back was uneventful, but not easy. The wind picked up sending clouds of ash and dust into the air. There were times when I thought I must surely choke to death. As the half moon began its rise into the clear night sky I returned to the southern fringe of Shooting Star Meadow.

I soon found Gondzor afloat near the edge of a shallow pool in the stream. "We are finding a similar condition at our infirmary too," he said with a worried look, after I had recounted Romla's message. "I will ponder this and tomorrow we will decide how to proceed. You go get some rest after your travel and good work."

Horns of Stone

SHORTLY AFTER daybreak I found myself at yet another meeting. Gondzor, in Zornova's absence, had called a meeting of the Council to discuss the illness that was afflicting so many of us. No one had any useful suggestions about what we should do.

"Have you tried mixing sky pilot with thistle?" asked Freeman the marten "It's what mom used to give us as a tonic when we felt down in the dumps. Nasty tasting stuff; but it sure made you feel better."

"Yes, we have tried that and many home remedies, but to no avail," replied Gondzor, obviously frustrated with our inability to come up with a viable solution.

It was then that Morgorgor spoke up, "It may be time to send someone to the Horns of Stone." After some murmuring among the other animals in attendance Morgorgor continued. "Yes I know that many of us remember the stories about the Horns of Stone told to us by the old ones long ago. Many of you may be too young to know about the horns, or of the terror and fear they bring to mind for many of us. But they are a place of truth, sometimes terrible truth, but truth nonetheless."

There was a long silence, broken only when Takatata, the ancient and tattered head of the lark clan, chirped up. "Morgorgor may be right. Perhaps we should consult Scragg, transmitter of the great wisdom from below. Maybe Scragg will be willing to speak this time. She said nothing when her wisdom was last consulted."

Morgorgor responded with fear and trembling, "Yes, I was a member of the group that was refused. Hegramond, Scragg's toady, had found our offering to be insufficient; she would not speak to us other than to shout, 'Be gone you miserable vermin' My dreams still remind me now and again of the terror of the silence that followed this malediction."

Scragg was an ancient cougar that had her lair in a dark and smelly cave in one of two craggy and isolated spires of crumbling stone, called the Horns of Stone. To get to this isolated lair surrounded by barren, treeless slopes, one had to travel past geysers and boiling mud pots, bogs filled with quicksand, and other pits and traps that could do in the unwary. There were no markers to guide the suppliants to this dark oracle. Many had turned back, and many others wished they had, or so it was rumored.

After some discussion, and because no better plan could be designed, it was decided that three suppliants were to be sent to the Horns of Stone to plead with Scragg and to seek her advice. I was to be one of the three. When our meeting ended I remained in place dumbfounded, I was so petrified with fear. Cawdor the crow and Brogoff the black bear were the other two emissaries chosen. The rest of the morning I felt hemmed in, surrounded by invisible clouds of doom and darkness weighing down upon me. Reluctantly, I organized my things in a small pack, while Brogoff did the same. While we prepared for this terrible journey the council continued to debate what it was that we should send as a gift or sacrifice to the ancient and terrible Scragg.

After a quick lunch Morgorgor handed me a small bag containing the sacrificial gift for Scragg. "Do not open this bag. Only Scragg, or perhaps her toady Hegramond, should open it and then decide whether or not she would condescend to answer our question. You must be polite, but not servile, when speaking to Scragg. And most important of all you must not show any fear. That old cougar hates fearful suppliants more than anything else. At least that's what the legends tell us. Good fortune on this journey; we will hold you in our hearts until you return."

"Morgorgor, I am so very scared," I blurted out. "Why couldn't you send someone else, perhaps Alexia? She is so strong and fearless, unlike me."

"Alexia is busy elsewhere. The council was unanimous in choosing you for this job. Just remember that we hold you in our hearts and you will be able to do all that you need to do," Morgorgor assured me.

I can't speak for Cawdor or Brogoff, but I departed from Shooting Star Meadow that afternoon with a heavy heart. Fear had gripped my mind and sucked the energy and strength from my limbs. Brogoff led the way northward towards the Horns of Stone while Cawdor flew above shouting directions to us. Though we had journeyed many times across these ridges and valleys, in its black and ruined condition it all looked strange. But, from above, Cawdor could see the essential features of the land and shout to us directing us more efficiently along our way. For two days we trekked northward across the Geyser District, the Paint Pots District, and then into Cougar District. Late on the second day as darkness surrounded us we came to a small stream of water. Cawdor descended to tell us that he could see the twin spires of the horns in the distance. From the opposite bank of the stream a barren rocky expanse sloped upward and ended in dingy clouds of steam that obscured our view of the Horns of Stone.

With weary limbs and heavy hearts we sat and ate in silence. Most likely Cawdor and Brogoff liked our mission to see Scragg as little as I did. We soon prepared for nightfall on the edge of this bleak and forbidding expanse of desolation. Thankfully weariness soon drew us into sleep.

My sleep was fitful, with dreams of falling into bottomless pits or stumbling into scalding mud pots, while being chased by some huge and howling beast. I awoke with a start when Brogoff shook me gently. Grumpily, I rubbed the sleep from my eyes; I had no desire to face the day to come. None of us seemed in the mood to talk. Each of us ate silently; each of us remained encased within the depths of our individually designed fears.

As sunlight began to filter through the mist we crossed the creek on a blackened, fallen log that provided access to the other side. Cawdor flew low above us, for otherwise he would have been lost in the clouds of ominous fog that seeped into every cranny and pit. As we drew away from the creek we found the going rougher. Splinters of jagged stone littered the rocky carapace of this miserable and deathly realm.

Cawdor shouted down from above, "Soon you will come upon a heap of immense stones; turn left there and follow what appears to be a narrow spine of stone. This will lead you safely between the mud pots."

We reached the heap of charred and blackened stone entangled within the fingers of swirling steam and mist. Brogoff had just turned left when all of a sudden there was a loud roaring, rushing sound followed by an explosion of steaming, scalding water. Brogoff was knocked off his feet by this watery explosion. He tumbled from the ridge into the noxious, sulfurous stench of the mud pots. Brogoff's howls pierced the fog-encrusted silence. Soon however, in spite of his pain, Brogoff was able to clamber back up onto the ridge. We retreated to the heap of stones to evaluate our situation. Brogoff was badly scalded, skin and fur melted away from his left side and hind legs. He could not go on. He was too badly hurt.

Cawdor, upon hearing Brogoff's howling cries descended swiftly, swooping down in a rush of black feathers. "Cawdor you must fly quickly for help. I will stay here and take care of Brogoff's immediate needs. Once that is done I will go on by myself" (Was I really uttering these words that sounded so brave and assured. I did not feel brave and assured.) Cawdor rose back into the fog and mist in search of help. I retraced my steps and crossed the stream searching for medicinal remedies that would be useful. Fortunately I found all four of these remedies after a brief search and hurriedly returned to Brogoff. Belladonna would help him sleep, arrowroot would ease his pain, spiders' webs, and lichen would stop the ooze of blood.

I ministered to Brogoff as best I could; then I managed to arrange his bedraggled, mud-caked form as comfortably as possible. Soon Brogoff quieted down and began to doze. With so many animals at risk there was no time to waste. I raced past the geyser that had spewed and startled Brogoff, then slowed down to clamber more carefully along the narrow ridge of stone. As I continued the ridge grew in height, but remained narrow and perilous. Below me on either side were burping mud pots spraying their mud-caked craters with multicolored clays. Then the ridge ended abruptly. I peered down into the seething pools of mud below. After a few moments I discerned a narrow ledge that angled down towards a lower and narrower ridge of stone forming a precarious causeway between the roiling pools and splattering cauldrons of hot mud.

After a brief moment of reflection, before I had time to think too long about the possible consequences of what I was about to do, I edged my way down the slanting ledge and onto the lower causeway-like ridge. I can barely remember how I made my way through the fog along that precarious ridge of stone, for fear gripped me tightly. After what seemed like hours of toiling onward a dark wall of stone loomed up before me. It was some time before I was able to make out a narrow ledge angling off to the right before disappearing into the mist, and now light rain. I could barely reach the ledge by standing on tiptoe. Several times I slipped on the rain-slick stone and almost fell to my death or to a tortured, painful injury.

Finally, after climbing several hundred feet upward and to the right, I emerged from the sea of fog and mist, onto a barren rocky plateau that sloped upwards towards two steep and dreadful prongs of stone. I gulped as I stared at these two ragged stone horns, frightened almost to immobility by the awesome dread that rose within me. Trembling slightly I forced myself onward, while holding in my heart the importance of this quest. I trudged slowly upwards toward these two unmatched tower-like spires. The top of the northernmost horn was blunted and singed, as though struck by some mighty bolt of lightning. Its shattered but still pointed shaft of stone lay at its base.

Where was the entrance to Scragg's den? No one back in the green expanse of Shooting Star Meadow had been able to give me clear directions. Morgorgor had suggested that I search the terrain near the base of the horns. Out of duty, more that real desire to find the entrance to the cougar's lair, I began to examine the tumbled mass of rock and debris. The entrance was certainly not easily found, I thought, after a half an hour of futile search. So I sat on a high stone and rested. While I rested I let my eyes wander over the lifeless stretch of weather-scarred stone. Once I was quiet, more from weariness than self-composure, I noticed a dark shadowed area about a hundred feet up the south flank of the southern horn. Well, there was no choice, I must climb up and see.

That was easier said than done. After several false starts I managed, by scrabbling over boulders and forcing my way through narrow crevasses between stones, to reach what indeed appeared to be the entrance to a cave. After waiting a moment to catch my breath and regain some shred of courage, I entered the darkness. I called out "Scragg, oh noble Scragg, I have come in search of your wisdom." My tremulous words bounced off the silent walls of the cave. But there was no answer. After proceeding some distance into the stench and quiet I tripped over some unseen object, fell, and darkness swallowed me.

I could not tell you how long I had lain unconscious. It might have been minutes or hours. I do not know. But I awoke to a soft sound nearby.

"Who is there?" I called out several times, with intervals between. But there was no answer. Moments later I felt foul breathes of air exhaled into my face. I reached out. Quickly I drew my paw back for I had touched something huge, cylindrical, and scaly. "Who are you?" I whimpered.

"Who wants to know?" was the velvet, breathy answer.

"I . . . I . . . I am Blinkers. I have come in search of Scragg." I whispered back into the blackness.

Inches from my face there appeared the huge gem-like eyes of an immense snake. The mouth opened, the tongue flicked in and out almost touching me. I drew back in terror. "I am Mendacitus, and I am ravenously hungry; even a jittery raccoon like you would fill my belly for some while."

"Oh please don't eat me. I have to see Scragg for words of wisdom and advice," I replied in a shaky voice I did not recognize as my own.

"Oh you have found Scragg already, you have. Stumbled over her you did, some time back."

"What do you mean? Is she still here so that I might bring my petition to her notice?" I asked.

"She is here, but no answers can she give you. It was her skull that brought you down. For more than four years she's been dead. And I mourn her loss, for no longer do the petitioners come to fill my belly. I hunger!"

"What about Hegramond?" I asked as I attempted to come up with some alternate plan.

"Hegramond departed this desolation onto the next world long before Scragg succumbed to age," was the syrupy response.

What must I do to avoid being eaten? I had no desire to be swallowed whole and then slowly digested within the scaly tube of snake. "Oh wise serpent, perhaps you are the holder of the wisdom that I seek."

"What if I am? What's in it for me?" shot back Mendacitus.

"Oh wily Mendacitus, if I spread word of your wisdom, the petitioners will seek you out, and fill your belly full, as in times past," I ventured.

"That is a delicious proposal indeed. But how am I to trust that you will do what you say?" rasped the soft snaky voice in return.

"There is no way to convince you. But I do know that you would find it difficult to slither safely back along the path I traveled to get here. It would be so much more satisfying if your dinner came to you. There would be no risk in that. But if you leave you might fall into the mud pots and die a horrid death!"

"Yes, yes, perhaps it is worth a try, though I am not convinced I can trust you. You would hardly do as a meal anyway; you are not much more than a scrawny wad of fur and bones, hardly worth the trouble to eat." He taunted as his tongue licked the rough edges of his gruesome, lip-less mouth. "Ask away then, and I will answer you as best I might!"

I briefly related to him the troubles of my fellow animals. "As you can see we have suffered much. Many among us have given in to despair and will not eat. So what can we do? What should we do?" I asked.

"Oh, that is very simple. You must go to the place where all things are made clear," answered Mendacitus. "And don't ask for any explanations, because none of them will I give you, for the oracle has spoken."

Though I did not know that I should accord this oracle with any value, I decided that it would be most politic not to say so at present. "Thank you oh Mendacitus," I responded with as much dignity as I could muster. "We will ponder your words well and act accordingly. Thank you for your esteemed wisdom. Before I leave I must give you a token of thanks sent by those whom I speak for." I took the small pouch from my pack and laid it on the floor.

"Open it, you foolish raccoon, for I am not equipped to untie the cords that would keep me from the gift within," rasped Mendacitus.

"Yes, oh great seer," I responded sheepishly. I had to admit that I was a little curious about what the pouch contained. Though

I was anxious to leave, I was able to force my paws to untie the knot and display this gift for Scragg and now Mendacitus.

"Well empty the pouch you stupid beast!" exclaimed the slithering Mendacitus.

It took a bit to get the knot undone for the cord had been tied securely to keep its contents secure, and the darkness made it difficult to see just what type of knot it was. Finally I untied the knot and opened the pouch. I could tell from the aroma that wafted forth just exactly what it was that the elders had sent as a gift. I doubted that Mendacitus would much appreciate the gift, for it was delicious mint. How was I to explain this gift in a way that would not anger Mendacitus and cause him to devour me before I could flee?

"Well, what is my present oh nimble-fingered one?" whispered Mendacitus.

"Well Mendacitus, seer and weaver of riddles, it is a rare and valuable herb much favored by the animals of the park," I answered.

"What's it good for?" asked the snake, his growing anger apparent.

My mind raced searching for some plausible explanation that would make it appear to be of some use for a snake. "Oh great and wily Mendacitus if you would take a sniff you could surely answer your own question."

"Its not some sort of poison is it?" queried Mendacitus.

"No, oh no, it is not harmful. I will take a good sniff first just to prove it is not dangerous for you," I responded. I stuck my nose into the pouch and inhaled. "See, I am still standing; I am not falling into some eternal sleep."

"Well, if it isn't poison, then what is it?" asked the baffled snake.

"It is a rich blend of very rare and valuable mint. If you want I could brew you a nice tea that will give you blissful dreams and raise your spirits," I answered.

"That is a silly gift; don't you have something better than that in your knapsack?" grumbled Mendacitus peevishly.

"Well possibly, though I am not really sure what I might have that a snake might desire" I replied. I dumped the contents of my pack onto the floor of the cave and said, "Do you see anything that would please you?"

The snake lowered his evil head with its saphire eyes, flicking his tongue in an out greedily. He used his nose to push about the items on the cave floor. Finally Mendacitus raised his head up and said, "What are these? They are a very curious item." Dangling from his teeth was a pair of reading glasses on a wire chain.

"Those are my old reading glasses," I said.

"What do they do?" asked Mendacitus.

"The glass lenses in the metal frame make the things I see, like words on a piece of paper, appear clearer and larger. I use them in my work back in Geyser District. But they don't help with seeing things at any distance," I responded.

"Put them on me, so I can see how they work," demanded Mendacitus.

So I held the glasses up in front of the great snake's eyes.

"These are marvelous," he responded. "They are the gift I desire."

"Then you may have them. But how will you wear them? I asked.

"Oh you will figure out a way to make them work for me," the snake hissed. Well I thought and I contemplated the possible ways to attach the glasses to the snake. It was not a simple problem since his ears did not stick out from his head. Eventually I came up with a plan.

"I think I have a solution," I said. Then I set to work. And by cutting the pouch into a long strip and bending the frames a bit I was able to make a band around his neck. Then I attached the chain to the band with the cord that had been used to close the pouch. I bent the earpieces so they would rest on the back of the snake's head. And with a bit of practice Mendacitus found that he could push the glasses up in front of his eyes using the tip of his tail and then push them back into the pouch fastened to the back of his neck.

"Splendid, mosssst sssplendid," hissed Mendacitus as he peered about through his new glasses. "Now be gone before hunger replaces my gratitude!"

Hurriedly, I gathered the remaining contents of my pack and shoved them back in, then fastened all the straps and buckles, and left as quickly as I could. I began to retrace my steps through the darkness of the cave. At least the serpent seemed to have told the truth about something, for I soon came upon the skeleton of a large feline. Now that my eyes were more accustomed to the dark I could indeed make out Scragg's rib cage and giant claws. I proceeded cautiously, for I thought perhaps Mendacitus might ambush me as I made my way towards the entrance to the cat's lair. Since I now relate to you my story you can conclude that indeed the snake did not act with such treachery, for I am here now and you are listening to my words.

I emerged from the cave's entrance almost without knowing it, for darkness had swallowed that barren terrain surrounding those great horns. In very fact, I almost tumbled to my death because I did not realize that I had exited the cave. As I was about to step over the edge and into nothingness, the moon rose and shed its feeble silver light on the abyss before me. It was too dangerous to travel further, so I encamped just inside the mouth of the cave until morning. I slept fitfully, for I feared the serpent as it slithered through each brief dream that night.

I awoke to mist and clouds, and with a bit of a smirk on my face, for I realized that I had unintentionally made it difficult for Mendacitus to swallow his victims. In order to keep the glasses from sliding along his body I had had to make the band I fashioned fit snuggly on the serpent's neck. The great snake would now be kept from eating anything much larger than an acorn without snapping the band and losing his prized glasses. I hoped I did not need to return to the Horns of Stone, for I would, no doubt, find Mendacitus in a vengeful mood.

Morning's thin, washed out light finally filtered through the fog. I retraced my steps without incident back towards where I had left Brogoff. I was worried about his condition, for he had been badly burned and was in great pain. I was relieved, as I approached the heap of stones to see Cawdor perched up high as sentinel. He cawed out loudly: "Blinkers! Blinkers has returned." Thicket's head rose up and she smiled at me as I approached; Jet flapped up onto a nearby boulder. So Cawdor had found help.

Behind a large boulder lay Brogoff, looking miserable, but better than before. Pudge, the marmot, was fussing around his immense patient, applying salves and ointments to areas of burnt flesh. Not bothering to look up at us Pudge grumbled, "Great you're back; please don't dunk me in a geyser. Glad you're back. Hope you got something worthwhile from that scraggly old Scragg."

"It's nice to see you too Pudge," I responded, "how is your patient?"

"Oh he'll live I guess. You didn't cook him quite long enough," he sniped. "Now get along quickly and take your message back to Gondzor and Zornova. Jet has been sent to guide you back to Shooting Star Meadow while Cawdor, Thicket, and I remain with Brogoff until he is able to travel."

After a brief rest and a quick meal I went on my way. Depressing thoughts surrounded me on my return journey. What Mendacitus had said seemed so very worthless. The council was bound to be disappointed with this vague oracle.

Meeting in the Meadow

I was surprised on my return to find representatives from most of the park districts assembled and awaiting my return. My heart sank, for it was clear that they placed much hope in what I had to tell them. Oh, what was I to do, for my mission to the Horns of Stone was surely a farce; nothing that Mendacitus had said would be of any help.

After a brief snack, for I had not stopped to eat on my return trek from the Horns of Stone, I was ready to go before the council and relate to the members the words of wisdom from the oracle. My tail twitched nervously as I awaited the end of Zornova's introductory words.

"As you know, Blinkers has just returned from the great oracle at the Horns of Stone. His journey was fraught with dangers. Even now Brogoff remains on the edge of the barrens recovering from severe burns. Remember that the wisdom of the oracle comes in the form of riddles, so don't be surprised if the meaning of the message is not readily apparent. Okay Blinkers, please come forward and tell us what was spoken to you," said Zornova as she stepped away to the side of the circle of assembled representatives.

With a great deal of apprehension I stepped to the center of the circle. Surrounded as I was by this circle of expectant eyes, it was almost impossible to keep my tail from twitching. But somehow I managed to still my tail. "Most esteemed representatives, I am honored to come before you. Before I speak to you the words spoken to me, I must tell you that they do not come from the mouth of the ancient and venerable Scragg, for she has been dead for several years."

A unison gasp was the response of the audience. Planga, a marten from Clear Creek Ranger District, was the first to call out: "If the words are not from Scragg, then how do we know they are to be trusted! How can we be sure that they are indeed oracular?" She was the first among many to question the value of what I would speak. I had my own doubts as well.

After briefly recapping my encounter with Mendacitus, I spoke the words he had given me: "You must go to the place where all things are made clear."

Silence followed these words, for indeed they did seem to sound wise, and like many oracular utterances the meaning was not immediately apparent.

"There are so many possibilities," said Zornova, "do any of you think you know what these words might mean?"

Morgorgor raised a paw. "Madame Ranger, it could be one of the many pools within the park that are deep and clear, like those up to the north?"

Then Planga the marten suggested, "It might be one of the high peaks, where on cloudless days you can see almost forever."

"Could it be the night sky, where we can see far into the heavens?" asked Colcol the mallard, from Big Sky District.

For some time animals suggested various possibilities. But, nobody seemed to do so with any deep and abiding convictions. Thus after much discussion that seemed to have no direction Zornova interrupted our confusion and bewilderment to call an end to the meeting. "All of you think on this. We need to reflect on these words, hold them in our hearts, until we can discern what it is they mean. We will meet tomorrow at dawn. By then we may have gained some insight and then decide what we must do."

The representatives moved slowly away from the circle. Gondzor was deep in conversation with Gormla. Morgorgor shambled away in silence. Many remained, as though transfixed, as they sought the answer to the riddle.

I was so exhausted from my journey that I quickly, well at least as quickly as possible given my sore feet, headed for my hollow log and sleep. Unfortunately, when I reached my log, I found that it had been transformed. The transformation was not, at least in my view, an improvement. My log now had little sprigs of wilted or wilting flowers hung about. There was an odd and not altogether pleasant odor wafting about. And, worst of all, Rutorina peeked from around a nearby tree trunk with a smarmy smile on her face. Oh no, I thought, I had forgotten about Rutorina's infatuation with me while I was focused on Scragg and the Horns of Stone. Rutorina had not forgotten!

"I see you have redecorated," I began somewhat meekly.

"Do you like it? Isn't it sweet and beautiful." She squealed with glee.

Actually that was not my response at all, but I did not wish to insult her. So I had to come up with some lame but kind response. "Most attractive, oh yes most attractive. Thank you for your efforts. But Rutorina, I am exhausted and I have a meeting at dawn tomorrow." I slumped down onto a bed of boughs and wished fervently for sleep.

Rutorina had other ideas. "But Blinkers, you must also be famished. You must keep up your strength my dear. I have prepared a light supper for you—oh you must eat. You are much too scrawny after all of your heroic adventures."

Well, I had no choice, and I was hungry. As politely as possible I endured a meal of grass seed and crushed pine nut pudding. It was all I could do to keep from throwing up. After I had eaten as much as I could stand, I said wearily, "Thank you Rutorina, but I can eat no more. What I need now is to sleep." That seemed to satisfy her for she waddled off with a silly smirk on her face.

I was just peering for the third time into a deep lake surrounded by mountains when the grumpy voice of Thimblewicket interrupted my dreams. "That's enough sleep for you, Sleeping Beauty," grumbled Thimblewicket. "Get along; the meeting will start in just a few minutes. Some pad you got here, who's your interior decorator? Phew, what is that stench? Now get along, no time to be lollygagging about, doing nothing, when there are important meetings to be had for the upper crust."

I yawned again as Thimblewicket shoved me towards the circle where the meeting was to take place. "Thanks, Thimblewicket, you can leave off with the sarcasm," I grumped as I stumbled, still half asleep, towards the group of animals milling about the meeting site we had used the day before. I stopped briefly at a small streamlet to wash the sleep from my eyes.

Zornova appeared a minute later and called the meeting to order. "Let us take a moment to collect ourselves before we continue our discussion from yesterday afternoon," she said. After several silent minutes she continued, "Last night my dreams were filled with visions of a long journey to a high mountain lake. At one point I was out in the lake on a small island. I looked into the deep waters. There below me, as I peered downward, I could see that the water clear as glass, I could see down almost forever to the distant bottom of the lake." There was a stunned silence from the other animals. Each was silent, not because Zornova's dream was so strange; rather it was because it sounded so familiar.

Morgorgor was the next to speak. "If steep cliffs and tall mountains, especially towards the south, surrounded your lake then I dreamed of the same lake.

"So did I!" exclaimed Planga. "The clear blue of the sky above was reflected on the lake's still surface. And—and it felt like I could see into heaven itself."

Other animals began to nod in confirmation. It soon became clear that each animal present had dreamed about this lake. Several animals' dreams were very distinct and clear, while other animals' dreams were hazy, but not so hazy as to make them different in their essentials.

This deep mountain lake was to the west, for Zornova and I remembered, from our dreams, traveling in that direction, towards the setting sun. Romla and Cawdor remembered crossing wide and rushing rivers on bridges made by humans. Wanda remembered watching Pabatackle slide down the steep snow into the deep lake. Keeble and Rittiticket remembered an attack by vicious dogs near a long fence.

Again Zornova interrupted the commotion and spoke, "Unless I hear anything to the contrary I plan to lead a party of eight towards this lake that appeared in our dreams. I take the continuity of these dreams as a sign of confirmation. The oracle has spoken and we must act. I will go and take with me those seven others who have had the clearest and most distinct dreams, or been seen within the dreams. I will take Romla the mountain lion, Cawdor the crow, Pabatackle the otter, Wanda the moth, Keeble the mule deer, Rittiticket the ground squirrel, and Blinklers."

Almost before I realized it my lips were moving, and I was saying, "But, but I can't go. I'm just so exhausted, my census report is unfinished, my notes and records are all a shambles; if I don't get them in order soon I shall never make sense of them. And you need to take those who are brave and love adventure, not a silly raccoon who is good at typing and taking notes." Then abruptly, I stopped, because I noticed that everyone was staring at me. If I could have blushed I would have at that moment. Then in a subdued tone I continued, "Oh forgive me, of course I will do whatever you would like me to do Zornova."

"Now that that is decided, we must prepare for our journey," Zornova said. "Romla, you and Rittiticket must gather the supplies we will need for the journey. Keeble, you and Wanda fetch Pabatackle and get him ready for this trek. Cawdor, you must search out Menke and Jet, to find out what they know of the way west. Perhaps they have flown over such rivers as those we crossed in our dreams. Blinkers, you come with me, there is business to take care of before we leave, and you are the only one fast enough to get it all done. We will leave tomorrow morning."

The Way West

B Y NOON the next day we were indeed on our way west. We would have begun our trek to the west, in search of the deep lake of our dreams much earlier, but for speeches and prayers and songs, all a part of our rousing sendoff.

I was still tired from my previous trek to the Horns of Stone, so each step was an effort. Cawdor flew above us searching for the best route for us to follow, the best places to cross roads and streams. Zornova headed our ground party crushing through the heavy brush, when necessary, to create a path for us to follow. Pabatackle, who had more energy than he knew what to do with, was next in line. He would dart one way then another sniffing and larking about. Every time we crossed a stream he must take a brief swim. Rittiticket was next. I followed Rittiticket and Romla, while Keeble brought up the rear. Wanda alternated between riding on Keeble back and hovering in the air above us. When Rittiticket began to show signs of weariness, he was given a lift up to either Zornova or Keeble's back for a ride and a rest.

The first part of our journey led us through the familiar parkland that we knew, where forests and open meadows alternated. Ridges of mountains had to be crossed as we pressed onward towards the park's western boundary. Once we left the park the going got tougher, for we were stepping out into unknown territory. Even though this made us, well everyone except Pabatackle, apprehensive, we knew that we must continue on, ever westward until we reached the deep lake. Soon after crossing the boundary we came upon herds of cattle grazing in the high country. We attempted to communicate with the cattle, but they paid us little heed as they chewed the meadow grasses with mute and mindless contentment. We also began to encounter an occasional fence, which was a particular annoyance for Zornova. Keeble could jump over them, the rest of us could climb through, but Zornova, though she was tough and strong, could do neither. So we had to search for gates, which provided long detours, or let Zornova reluctantly push down the fence so we could continue on. Every once in a while, as we continued our westward journey, we came across an isolated human dwelling.

After two days of such travel Cawdor took a longer scouting trip ahead to get a better idea of what we would encounter over the next several days. While we rested, or in Rittiticket's case, collected food for our next day's journey, we tried not to think of the dangerous parts of our communal dream, like the attack of the dogs. Late that afternoon, just after a brief thunderstorm Cawdor returned.

"We have two choices," he began, after taking a brief rest "If we head northwest we will encounter range after range of mountains; if we head south we will encounter a dry and arid plateau. Travel though the mountains might be friendlier, but the travel would be slower. The arid plateau would give us quicker travel, but provide little food and even less water. Whichever way we chose we would be forced to cross the great and roiling river. But for the near future there is only a shallow river to cross."

After deciding to take the quicker route we gathered our meager belongings and set out at a rapid clip, Rittiticket riding on Zornova's back. Cawdor swooped down when he needed to pass along important information about the path we should follow. As the sun was dropping below the western mountains we reached the first river. Zornova ferried Rittiticket across. The rest of us got across on our own. Pabatackle swam, I hopped from rock to rock, and Romla crossed over on a fallen tree that had formed a bridge.

After a good hearty drink we moved up into the forest to make camp before darkness settled upon us. Now that we were out of the park we took turns on watch so that we might not be surprised by either humans or tamed animals. The world beyond the park was not so safe as that inside it. I had first watch that night. When the moon was straight overhead I woke Romla, for her turn on guard duty followed my own. After what seemed like all too short a time of sleep Keeble awakened me and we were on our way again after a quick breakfast. We encountered nothing of note during the day. But Cawdor pushed us on after dark so that we could cross under a major four-lane highway under cover of darkness. We were apprehensive as we approached the roar of cars and huge trucks speeding along, headlights dazzling the night. We crossed under the highway where it traversed a bridge across a small creek. The large metal culvert was just big enough for Zornova. The rest of us had no difficulty. However, the hoof beats of the ungulates echoed off the walls of the culvert, creating an eerie sound.

The terrain that came after the great highway was mostly flat and barren. There was little to drink or eat. We often stopped to rest in the middle of the day because the hot sun beat down on us without interruption. We rose as soon as it was light and then, after our mid-day siesta, traveled until it was too dark to travel safely. Actually, for me, travel at night was just fine, but the same could not be said for Zornova and Wanda. To keep our spirits up we would chant or sing softly as we walked. We were fortunate, when we had not had water for two days, to run across several grazing antelope, early one morning.

Zornova, her mouth parched with thirst, noticed how these antelope, unlike the cattle we had encountered, stared at us with questions and curiosity. So she risked speaking to them "Could you direct us to water, for we are unfamiliar with this land?"

The closest antelope peered at us with his intelligent eyes, and then responded, "I will do better than that, for I see that you are weary. If you will follow me I will take you there myself. Lets go." He then led us to a small water hole about two miles distant.

Once we had all drunk our fill and were feeling much better he introduced himself. "I am Zeecor Manata, I have lived on these open plains my whole life and have never seen a traveling band such as yours. Where are you from and where are you headed."

Zornova introduced herself and then the rest of us to Zeecor Manata. "You have been a great help to us. We thank you for your hospitality and assistance. We are from the great park to the east, where the mountains rise up and boiling waters spew from the earth. We are headed for a crystal clear lake in the high mountains to the west. Oracular words have been spoken to us and we seek to follow their directions. Our friends and families have suffered from a great fire, and a plague of despondency that followed quickly on the heels of the fire. We welcome any help you might give on the best route westward."

Zeecor, without hesitating, responded, "I will act as your guide, for I have run to the east and the west, up unto the feet of the mountains. I know this land and I see the suffering of your friends and families in your eyes. I can take you to the very edge of the great tumbling river. From there westward you must find you own way, or find another willing guide."

"Whenever you are ready to lead, we will follow," Zornova replied.

For what seemed like weeks we followed the noble antelope Zeecor Manata across the endless waves of grassy slopes. He skirted the edges of alkali flats and led us to the cool springs hidden in obscure canyons. To us the landscape was one monotonous repeating image. But to Zeecor Manata each place had its name, each slope sang to him its particular melody. We kept clear of towns, avoided ranches and passed days that seemed to us much alike.

One morning, however, we came upon a newly erected line of fence that had not been there the last time Zeecor Manata had traveled this way. We followed the fence south for several hours. Near a small spring and three sparse trees we settled down to rest, for abundant waves of heat rose from the land almost suffocating us. Cawdor, perched in the upper branches of the southernmost tree, cawed out loudly startling us awake. A pack of nondescript, ragtag hounds emerged from an empty irrigation ditch and headed towards us snarling, teeth shining in the sunlight. There must have been fifteen or sixteen of them; I did not take the time to count. I snatched up Rittiticket who was resting next to me and clambered up the nearest tree. Zornova awoke quickly to face the dogs with Romla at her side. Keeble and Zeecor Manata got several of the dogs to chase after them. Zeecor Manata and Keeble ran slowly enough to keep these dogs on their trail, but fast enough to avoid the snapping jaws and sharp teeth.

Rittiticket found a refuge high in the tree near Wanda, and I went back to fight. Zornova called out to the yapping dogs who were somewhat intimidated by her size, "Why do you attack us? If we intrude upon your territory we will gladly leave, just let us go in peace." But the dogs only snarled and barked and spoke not a word to us. Their eyes, like those of the cattle, had a dull and clouded appearance, reflecting limited comprehension. Soon we were surrounded. Zornova faced south, Romla north, Pabatackle east, while I faced west. The circling, yapping dogs worked their way closer, alternating advance and retreat. Finally one lunged at

Pabatackle, who feinted to the right, twisted around and bit the dog on his back leg. Yowling with pain the dog retreated, looking surprised that such a small creature could pack such fight in him. The next attack was in my direction. As this dog charged I jumped upon its back, digging my claws into its back and shredding its floppy ears with my teeth. We rolled and tussled in a heap, until he too left us. Meanwhile Zornova, using her horns, had tossed two or three dogs high up into the noonday heat. Two other dogs fled with deep claw marks given them by Romla. Two more dogs lunged forward. The first was swatted away by Romla and the second was catapulted from Zornova's horns. This second dog did not move again after it hit the ground with a heavy thud.

Having had enough, the dogs slunk away, but not too far away. Clearly this pack intended to wear us down until they gained some success. And they were really mad at us now that one of their number lay dead on the hard earth and several more were whimpering with pain. It was then that Zeecor Manata and Keeble returned, having exhausted the dogs that chased them.

After a brief discussion we decided that we must leave immediately, for the dogs would surely worry us until we became too weary to continue fighting. So we moved out in close formation with Zeecor Manata and Zornova leading the way, then Rittiticket and Wanda atop Keeble's back, followed by Pabatackle and myself, with Romla bringing up the rear. Almost as soon as we set out the dogs began again to harass us, at least until another dog limped away after misjudging Romla's speed and strength. Most of the dogs continued to follow us, though at some distance from Romla, our rear guard.

"We must find some safety or we will spend a dreadful night when they attack us under cover of darkness," said Zornova, clearly concerned for all of us. "Do you know of any way out of our dilemma, Zeecor Manata?"

After a moment's reflection Zeecor said, "Yes I do. While the dogs were chasing me I scouted out the path we must take from here. You must travel for a while without me, perhaps an hour or so. The fence ends in half a mile. From there follow the wheel ruts that lead southwest until you reach a dry streambed. Follow the streambed southward, through a narrow canyon, until the canyon opens out into a wide meadow. I should have help for you by the time you reach the meadow. I must get going quickly."

Soon Zeecor Manata was out of sight. Our dispirited party followed Zeecor's directions. By the time we reached the streambed several dogs were off to the right and to the left about a hundred yards out; the rest of the pack remained about the same distance behind us. Now and again two or three dogs would move in closer to assess our condition. We began to worry that we might be trapped within the narrow confines of the canyon that loomed up on either side of us. After several hours of following the streambed we began to weary. Almost immediately the dogs moved, attacking from all sides. In the tumble and turmoil that followed all of us prayed that Zeecor Manata had not forgotten us. Even though Zornova's hooves had crushed two more dogs and many more bore Romla's claw marks, the attack did not abate. Pabatackle and I had retreated into a narrow crack in the canyon wall along with Wanda and Rittiticket. Keeble sped out towards the meadow drawing away two of our attackers to follow her. Three dogs were stuffing their jaws into our narrow crack, biting and snarling and we clawed and snapped back. Zornova and Romla stood their ground, but both were tiring from the onslaught.

It was at that moment that we sensed a change, heard a strange sound. Then hundreds of antelope charged across the meadow driving the dogs before them. Zeecor Manata had rescued us and driven away our enemies. Once the dogs had scrambled off we crept forth from our refuge in the crack and stared in wonder at the circle of antelope that now gave us the protection we needed.

Zornova was too tired and winded, so I thanked these strangers who had come to our rescue. "We thank you from our hearts for your timely rescue. We thank you also on behalf of those who depend on the success of our mission. There is no way that we can ever repay you for what you have done. The best we can do is to hold your images and actions in our hearts and then share with those we meet and those at home the tales of your bravery."

Zeecor Manata spoke next. "These are the Cana Vahata tribe of antelope, and this" he indicated with his head, "is my old friend Cawalla Pan their leader."

That evening was spent in sharing stories with our new friends. We learned that long ago Zeecor Manata had traveled this way. Cawalla Pan and Zeecor Manata, after a spirited session of charging at one another with prongs lowered, decided to become friends rather than continue fighting. We would learn before the night was over that the Cana Vahata, or at least a contingent of them, would accompany us as far as the great river. We were able to relax and sleep more deeply that night knowing that the next portion of our journey would be with friends.

Stories and Otter Business

WHEN THE sun found me the next morning my whole body ached from the fighting and the tension of the previous day. My eyes opened slowly, and for a moment I was startled to see all of us surrounded by hundreds of antelope munching contentedly on thin silver-green stalks of grass. Then I remembered the rescue, and that I was safe, at least for now. I yawned and stretched to ease stiff muscles. My belly ached with hunger so I began searching for my breakfast in this unfamiliar terrain. Not far away Pabatackle and Rittiticket lay curled up together next to Romla, who was awake but hesitated to waken her small companions' sleep. Keeble and Zornova had joined the antelope to graze while Wanda flitted from flower to flower and Cawdor circled the clouds above us.

We set out later than usual and traveled slowly. We rested as usual at midday when the sun beat down upon us. By late afternoon we were facing the sun through rolling grasslands, cut through by occasional ravines or dry creek beds. Just before evening we departed from all but about twenty of the antelope. Cawalla Pan and one contingent of antelope came along with us while the rest of the herd scattered in small groups and headed back to their summer grazing lands.

Cawdor had warned us that we were approaching another great highway, and Cawalla Pan confirmed his report.

"We must go beneath the great highway using an underpass that we should reach tomorrow evening," announced Cawalla Pan. "It should be a dark night with just a sliver of moon to give us light. There should be little traffic on the narrow road that will lead us beneath the highway."

That night we rested while Cawalla Pan regaled us with stories of his youthful adventures with Zeecor Manata.

"Zeecor, do you remember the time we visited Boise? Now that was an adventure!" chuckled Cawalla Pan.

"I sure do remember that foolishness, but it makes a good story nonetheless, so why don't you share it with our new friends," Zeecor Manata replied.

"Well," Cawalla Pan began, "it was late summer and the grasslands were parched. We had been heading slowly west exploring the foothills of the mountains, staying clear of the towns and ranches, when we noticed how green it was down below us near the middle of this great conglomeration of humanity. We didn't give it much thought, but continued on westward. A few weeks later when food had become sparse and more difficult to find Zeecor up and says, 'I bet there is plenty of good grass to eat in that city we passed some time back. Let's go and check it out.' But Zeecor I said, 'you know that would only lead to trouble.' And you said 'has that ever stopped us before.' And I said 'no! I don't guess that it ever has.'

"So we ambled back towards the city. It took us about two days to get back. But over those two days we schemed and plotted about the best way to get to that green grass. Late one evening we arrived in the foothills above the city. We stared down at the sparkle of city light; we commented on just how magical it all looked from up here in the hills. We spent the next day studying the terrain and picking out the route we would take and discussing the best time to set out and return. And before long our plan was honed and as shaped and beautiful and perfect as any plan could be. Or so we thought!

"Just as the sun was dropping down into the western mountains we set out. We had already edged up as close to the outskirts of the city as we dared. We slipped down through dark yards, avoiding dogs and fences. It was not long before some of the lights began to go off inside of buildings and houses and the street were pretty much empty of cars. So now we became brave and made our way along the streets, darting behind trees and sheds when the headlights of a car headed in our direction. Once a couple of big dogs set up a ruckus, and we had to scamper quickly away through a wide-open space filled with upright slabs of stone. We surprised a couple of joggers; they had waited until the night air had cooled the dark city. Anyway, as we headed towards the center of the city the houses got closer together, and then we got to the part that had buildings with no lawns, just street. Everything was paved, so it became more difficult to walk quietly. Our hooves clacked softly on the pavement, but we were determined not to give up our goal.

"Soon great buildings of stone and glass surrounded us. We were beginning to get a bit anxious and doubt the wisdom of our venture. Actually, we never thought it was a sensible or wise thing to do, but we pressed on. Soon we reached our goal, a lush green lawn with large buildings and large parking areas nearby. However, to our dismay, we found the grass cropped off close to the ground. Those silly humans had used some kind of machine to cut the grass, rather than allow it to grow tall and lush like any sensible antelope would. Even though the grass was short, it was green and we did our best to consume as much as we could.

In our eagerness to gorge ourselves we forgot that we were in the middle of the city. We paid no attention to the sky, which had begun to show the first hints of morning light. Just as we had decided to skedaddle, we found that our venture had not gone unnoticed. Pulling up to a nearby curb was a large truck. Soon humans with some kind of strange apparatus were (as we would later learn) filming us. Since our intention had not been to make a spectacle we edged slowly away from the grass and sought out the quieter streets. Fortunately there was not much traffic on this particular morning. The only places people seemed to gather in any great number were near the buildings with pointed towers.

"The oddest thing, and we almost missed it, was seeing ourselves cropping the grass. I happened to glance into a house as we headed for the hills. And there on the side of a bright glowing box was a picture of Zeecor and me, chomping away. I called Zeecor back to look and he almost died of surprise. A voice emanating from the box said 'early this morning Idaho's capital city became aware of two nightly visitors on the lawn adjacent to the State Capitol. Now its time for our daily weather update; it looks like we will have another hot sunny Sunday.' At that moment a human came into the room and noticed us peering through the window, so we moved on nonchalantly, as if it was not unusual for antelope to visit state capitals.

"Not long after that we noticed a large van, with the words Animal Control plastered on all sides. 'We are being followed' whispered Zeecor. 'I think we need to keep a low profile from here on out.' It was silly of Zeecor to think that two antelope could keep a low profile in a city. Soon what seemed silly became a real threat. We noticed, after a few more minutes, that there were three vans coming towards us from different directions. 'We are being surrounded! I said. We gotta get out of here, and quickly.' We picked up our pace and the three vans sped up. Even when we changed direction the vans kept on coming. It was then that we made a mistake and bolted through an opening in a fence. One van pulled up behind us and blocked the opening. We saw another opening in the fence on the other side of a large field divided by white lines. We made for that opening on the run, but just when we were a hundred feet away, up pulled another van blocking that opening.

"Now we were really beginning to worry. It was then that I spied a small opening off to the right. We changed direction just in time to see the third van pull up and block our final avenue of escape. Humans were setting up nets, and dogs on leashes began to howl and bark. 'We are going to have to jump the fence,' I said. 'It's a mighty high fence,' said Zeecor, 'but we have no choice.' We turned and feinted in one direction and then circled quickly and galloped downhill and headed directly for the fence. We jumped. Both of us brushed our hind hooves on the fence top, but we cleared it. We gave up the nonchalant act and ran as fast as we could towards the edge of the city and never looked back.

"Think of all the tales you are already collecting, stories to tell when you return to the park. Stories are about who we have been, and who we are, and who we are becoming; without them life would be a drab and mundane collection of endless monotonous days," said Zeecor. "Though we could continue on all night swapping stories we need to be rested for tomorrow's journey, so let's call it a night."

I was asleep as soon as I rested my head on my paws. And all too soon Zornova was prodding me awake.

Early the next morning I was walking again, along with the rest of our party, still half asleep. Another clear blue and cloudless sky rose above us as the sun crept up into its full height in the sky. Nothing of particular note occurred during the day and our passage under the great highway was almost without incident. While we waited until nightfall in a grove of trees behind a ramshackle barn, long ago abandoned by its occupants, Pabatackle discovered a motorcycle parked inside one of the horse stalls. Up he goes and hops onto the thing and pretends to be racing down the highway. Soon he noticed a motorcycle helmet hanging on the handlebars, so he puts in on, though of course it was much too big for his almost brainless head. Again he is messing around, poking at dials and switches when he notices a bright shiny key. So he turns it while grasping one end of a handlebar. Such a roar of noise followed, and Pabatackle was so startled that he falls to the ground.

Out from another stall staggers a human, half-asleep, but looking mighty angry. He sees Pabatackle still wearing the helmet, up on his hind legs peering at him.

That human turns the key, quieting the noisy machine, throws an empty can at Pabatackle and staggers back into the stall he had earlier emerged from muttering, "It must be the whisky that's causing these hallucinations, that's the last time I'm ever going to drink that stuff." Once the human had disappeared, Pabatackle hopped back up onto the motorcycle seat and reaches toward the key. A low growl and a deep throated "Don't even think about turning that key again," from Romla put an end to Pabatackle's hijinks.

By the time it was dark there was no traffic on the small road that crossed under the wide highway. So in groups of three or four we scurried beneath and disappeared into the darkness on the opposite side. After another hour of travel by slim crescent moonlight we stopped.

Cawalla Pan announced, before we burrowed once more into night's sleep, "Tomorrow we will reach the great river. We of the Cana Vahata are honored to have traveled with such brave seekers after wisdom and truth. Zeecor and I will cross the bridge with you and then return. Cawdor has already flown ahead to scout out the territory through which you must travel." I don't know about the rest of my companions from the park, but I was feeling sad. I had felt cared for traveling with these proud and sturdy antelope. It gave me hope to know that we could be so well treated by strangers. It gave me fear to know that we would again be heading into unknown regions alone and without a guide to lead us. My sleep was filled with strange dreams of floating down rivers, of climbing snowy mountains and of a deep, an endlessly deep, lake.

I awakened to Cawdor's harsh cawing; he had just returned from his scouting trip to the west. Cawdor and Zornova spoke for a while before coming to us with the plan for the day's journey. So after foraging for breakfast we set out again. As we traveled we got occasional glimpses of a great river to the south of us. As morning mingled with afternoon we saw ahead of us how the river formed a great lake. By late afternoon we saw a barrier in the river, something Cawalla Pan called a dam. We were frightened occasionally as airplanes raced across the sky, and positively petrified when they did so very close to the ground. By late evening we could see a narrow bridge up ahead that crossed the river.

Near nightfall we stopped within view the bridge. Zeecor Manata and Cawalla Pan ambled down closer to the bridge to check things out, while we rested and chatted with our escort of antelope. It was a sad time for we did not want to leave them, nor the safety they provided us. Our chatting was punctuated by Pabtackle's exclamations of glee.

"I can hardly wait," he said, as he danced "I haven't had a good swim in ages. Such I big river, it will be great fun to dive and swim. I can't wait; I can't wait, I can't wait."

"You will just have to wait for a while longer," interrupted Zornova. "There will be no swimming any time soon."

"I know, I know we have to wait until dark to go to the great river, but then I will swim," replied Pabatackle with exasperation.

"Not in this river you won't, you silly otter. You would be swept away from us in no time and we would never see you again; this river would eat you alive," retorted the grave Zornova.

Before Pabatackle could whine and protest any further the air was cut by the sound of a shot. We jerked our heads around to face the bridge and noticed that an old truck had pulled up just this side of the bridge. Two men with guns were standing next to it. Cawalla Pan and Zeecor Manata were headed across the road and then west, to draw attention from us. We moved silently down into a low area that would keep us from view. Cawdor stayed up at the top of the ridge with Wanda so that he could monitor the movements of the two men and warn us should they move in our direction.

We waited for an hour or so, but the men showed no signs of leaving. Instead of going away they seemed intent on staying where they were. They built a fire and were drinking from cans. This was not good.

Obviously frustrated with this delay, Zornova finally said, "I'm going to charge in there and run them off."

Keeble shook her head and replied, "I don't think that's a good idea. You could be shot, and we need you to lead us onward to the lake."

Then Romla volunteered, "I could sneak up and scare the wits out of them with a loud growl."

Finally Wanda who had been flitting about wildly got a chance to speak "I have a better way and none of us will be hurt. Trust me I have it figured out, but I need to get to work on my plan so that we can move ahead quickly."

Before anyone could ask Wanda what she was going to do, she was gone. We crept a bit closer to see what would happen. For a while nothing obvious happened. Then a large humming sound and a darkish cloud descended upon the two men. They started slapping and waving their hands about. After about a minute of this frenetic behavior they picked up their rifles, got in their truck and drove away. Wanda had obviously got help from the local mosquito population. Then we noticed her perched on Keeble's ear chuckling.

"Wanda that was brilliant; it was also funny," snickered Pabatackle.

Cawdor circled around for a few minutes before reporting that all was clear and that we could cross the bridge. The roar of the great river was immense and scary. First Cawalla Pan and Zeecor Manata crossed the bridge. Then Zornova and Keeble with Rittiticket on her back ambled across the high bridge. Pabatackle and I with Wanda flitting above brought up the rear. It was then that it hit me. Zeecor Manata and Cawalla Pan would be turning back. There was anxious churning in my stomach as I remembered how much safer we had all been with them to guide us.

Our good-byes were brief but heartfelt. Cawalla Pan promised to keep a patrol in the area to watch for us on our return journey. Tears filled our eyes when we went our separate ways. Cawalla Pan and Zeecor Manata headed back over the bridge and we plunged into the darkness, for we needed to put some distance between the bridge and us. We traveled for some time in silence, nobody wanting to reveal the sadness he or she felt. We walked quietly for five miles before finding a protected spot to sleep and wait for the next day to arrive.

Back in Marmot Meadow

WE ALL felt depressed, a bit down in the dumps. Even Pabatackle seemed to have no inclination to clown around. Finally Wanda spoke about what was bothering us. "What we really want to know is what's happening back in Marmot Meadow. We want to know how our friends and families are getting along. We want to watch the green shoots of grass and meadow plants sprout from the ashes and return our home territory back to the way we remember it."

"You are right about that," responded Zornova. "It wouldn't hurt to talk about our homesickness a bit."

"I miss grazing with the other deer. I miss frolicking in the meadows as the sun drops below the western mountains," murmured Keeble.

"I miss the wonderful water, the abundant lakes and streams," muttered Pabatackle despondently.

"I miss my daughter Zenja and my mate Trankor," sighed Romla.

"I miss being at the center of all that activity, all the busyness of the office that a dispatcher has to contend with," mused Rittiticket.

"I miss the order and security of my office. I like it better when I know what's going to happen and what I need to do," was what I said. "What about you Wanda?"

"Oh, I miss the abundant wildflowers, and I miss Gimlet and many of my other friends," answered Wanda.

"Besides the bison Tennial, I miss the lush green grass and the other certainties of everyday life," contributed Zornova. "I do not like bearing the weight of responsibility which all of us share.

A few more snippets of conversation followed. But soon Pabatackle and then others drifted off to sleep. Before long I was sleeping deeply myself. I floated from one pleasant dream into another seamlessly. Then my pleasant dream began to turn into a nightmare. I was walking beside endless rows of animals—marmots, badgers, ravens, deer, and many others. All were clearly very ill, very close to death. Many of the faces I saw were faces I knew. I looked away from my friends who were sick and dying, because I could stand it no more. And, not far away, was Gondzor, pacing back and forth, something he had never done when I was around him at the Geyser District headquarters. I could tell that he was very worried, uncertain about how to deal with all of the pain and suffering he saw before him.

Then, with typical dream-world logic, my dream shifted and I found myself viewing a completely different scene. Morgorgor was pointing a paw at Nelia the black bear. I could hear Morgorgor say, "Nelia was seen killing and then devouring Conga and Spats, two rabbits. She was eating flesh. She let her hunger drive her to kill and eat her friends, knowing all the while that within the park such brutal behavior is forbidden. Gondzor, as deputy ranger, you must decide what to do."

"I don't know what's to be done," moaned Gondzor. Clearly he was overwhelmed. "I can help you, I can help you," emerged from my mouth. Then it all disappeared as Keeble prodded me with her right front hoof.

"Wake up, Blinkers, you must be having a bad dream. Wake up Blinkers" she repeated.

I woke to find seven sets of eyes staring back at me.

Wanda spoke next. "Were you back in the park in your dream? Was Nelia on trial for killing and eating Conga and Spats?"

"Yes, that could have been what I dreamed about. But how could you know what happened in my dream?" I queried.

Wanda answered, "You were not the only one dreaming of our home the park. In fact all of us, after our talk about our homes before we slept, have traveled back to the park in our dreams. Not only that, but our dreams are frightful and worrying."

"Then there are two things I think we must do," interjected Keeble. "We must press on rapidly towards our goal, this deep clear lake to the west. We also must hold our homeland in our hearts and ask the great creator to bring wisdom to Gondzor and other leaders who are left behind."

"Yes, you are right, but will that make us feel any better and worry any less?" asked Romla.

After a pause Zornova responded, "We may not feel better or worry less if we pray. But if we open our ears while we pray we may receive some word or feeling of peace granted us by the great creator, which will ease our hearts and minds as we journey on."

Very quietly Wanda began a prayer. "Oh creator of the earth, the universe, and all that is good, take care of those we have left behind. Heal those who are ill and give wisdom to the leaders who seek to care for them. Allow us to trust your love for us so that we may journey onward unencumbered by worries great or small. Keep us safe as we travel." Others of us added to what Wanda had begun. By the time we finished our prayers a faint glow had appeared in the east as the sun's light began to spread through a new day. We felt better, though some doubts and worries remained.

We spent the morning traveling westward through gullies and over ridges. We rested in the afternoon before trekking onward in the evening until we were weary and it was dark. I was almost afraid to sleep again for fear of more depressing and anxiety-provoking dreams. But my weariness overwhelmed me and I slept. Again I dreamed of the park; I dreamed of Marmot Meadow and of animals in rows. But they seemed to sleep in peace, as though something had brought some healing to them. And, my one view of Gondzor showed him caring for two ground squirrels. He did not appear to be hassled or worried any more.

When I woke the next morning we shared our dreams. We found that our dreams communicated a sense of greater peace. We were heartened and comforted by what we had learned as we slept.

The Extreme Stream

A s THE sun appeared and then rose, a cloudless sky greeted us. In every direction, dry and endless plains spread around us—or so it seemed. Soon we were on our way west, the sun warming our backs as we walked. As morning progressed waves of heat seemed to radiate up from the ground and ripple into the emptiness of the sky. Near noon we took a break near some small and scrubby trees and the bank of a dry creek bed.

"We must travel at night," said Keeble "for this heat will surely kill us. Maybe Romla or Blinkers can scout out the terrain ahead and keep us going in the right direction. Cawdor can scout out the big picture during the day."

Resignedly, Zornova answered, "Yes, that is what we must do. We will make the best of this little bit of protection until late afternoon. Then we will set out again."

We dozed fitfully until the sun began to drop towards some distant mountains to the west. We found water after several hours of trekking across this baked and almost barren landscape with its sparse grass and clumps of sage. Slowly we ascended towards the mountains Cawdor had told us we must climb; he said it was the best route so we followed him until it became too dark for him to see what lay below him. Romla, with her excellent night vision, scouted out the best ways after that. We were heading for a small trickle of a creek that Cawdor had spotted earlier in the evening. There was thick grass at the creek's edge to provide food. It was rough going for Keeble and Zornova, especially when the terrain became rocky. Even though we could not always be certain that we were headed in the right direction the night was cool and we felt refreshed by a light breeze.

After many hours of walking we came to the stream we had been searching for just as the sun rose to the east. Each of us drank deeply from the stream before we looked for food. Once our hunger was satisfied we looked for places to lie down.

"Blinkers, you have the first watch," yawned Zornova, just as I was about to curl up under an overhanging rock. I clambered up to a higher spot that would give me a better view of all approaches and waited. Before long clouds began moving across the sun, the wind picked up and large, heavy drops of rain began to fall. I rejoiced in the rain; I was sick of the endless and arid expanses across which we had traveled to reach our present resting place. Soon, in my exposed position I became soaked and then sodden. A blustery wind drove the rain sideways, pelting me, first from one direction and then another. I began to shiver. I almost ceased to pay attention. As I huddled up against some rocks that afforded me virtually no protection from the weather my gaze, almost by accident, dropped to the streambed, down near the base of the rise on which I had perched myself.

What had been a mere trickle when we arrived had now become a raging torrent.Soon the resting place of my companions would be flooded. I rushed down the hill to awaken my sleeping friends who had huddled beneath an overhang of rock that projected out from a steep cliff on the opposite side of the stream. I could no longer reach my companions. I shouted and shouted, but they did not waken. Oh how was I to warn them when they slept so soundly? Then it occurred to me that I might awaken one of them if I could just hit them with the pebbles that were readily abundant at my feet. It took me several tries, but finally I managed to lob one stone high and far enough that it rattled Pabatackle's skull.

Quickly he realized the danger posed by the rising stream. He awakened the others and they hurried warily along the opposite bank to higher ground. But once there they realized that Wanda was not with them. Pabatackle rushed back down to the rock overhang, but could not find her anywhere. He then began to search the surrounding area until he noticed a rocky outcrop, out in the stream about twenty feet or so downstream from the overhang. There she had flattened herself against one wall of a small crevice hoping not to be blown away by the wind. She could not fly through such wind and rain; it was too much for her small wings. Water had long ago surrounded the outcrop of stone and would soon rise above the crevice in which she had sought refuge.

Pabatackle realized that something must be done immediately. And since he was the best swimmer in the group, he realized that he must be the one to attempt a rescue. He ran back upstream and plunged into the swollen stream. He disappeared beneath the foaming torrent of water. Soon his head popped above the water about ten feet upstream from the outcrop. Clutching at the fringes of the outcrop he pulled himself up out of the raging waters. Immediately he extricated the reluctant Wanda from her small cavern. Knowing that she would be unable to cling to him for long and not be washed away forever, he gently placed her in his mouth and lunged back into the water. Every so often Pabatackle's head emerged above the white water. I scrambled along the opposite bank, following his progress from the shore.

It was then that I noticed a fallen snag hanging out over the swift flowing current, about twenty yards downstream. Without thinking, I darted out along the snag, hoping it would not give way beneath me. I searched the water for that silly otter. I saw a dark and rising form in the water below me, so I grabbed at it and held on with all my strength. Slowly Pabatackle pulled himself up onto the gnarled snag. He spat Wanda out into my waiting paws where I held her gently until we could make our way gingerly back along the snag to the bank. Pabatackle hopped onto the rocks. I followed him quickly. Just as my left hind paw reached the solid stone the snag teetered and the fell into the stream. Almost immediately it was driven against a great boulder. With a resounding crash it was shattered into myriad splinters.

Soon the three of us found shelter high up above the bank in a small cave. Wanda, once she began to dry off, began to move and stretch her wings tentatively. It was soon clear that she was not injured.

Wanda, her voice almost inaudible, quivered, "Pabatackle thank you, you were a fool to risk your life to save one small moth, but I shall never forget what you have done for me. And Blinkers, you were almost as big a fool, climbing out on that old snag of a tree. I owe my life to you both."

Since we were on the opposite bank of the stream from Zornova and the others we could not rejoin them at present. All three of us were cold and exhausted so we huddled together for warmth while we waited for the storm to abate. Our snoozing was occasionally interrupted by thunderclaps. Dark storm clouds soon merged with night's darkness. We slept knowing that as soon as the storm ceased Cawdor would search for us. In the middle of the night, small feet scampering past my ears awakened me. I heard a small voice muttering.

"What a grand great ugly oaf! How rude of this lout to block the entrance to my burrow," squeaked a diminutive voice.

It was then that I noticed the moonlight reflecting on two small beady eyes belonging to a golden-mantled ground squirrel. It scampered back and forth just a foot or two from my nose, obviously agitated about something.

"The great lout! Of all the nerve," the small voice continued.

"Is there something I can do for you?" I whispered, not wanting to awaken my sleeping companions nor startle the small creature.

"Well, yes, of course there is, otherwise I wouldn't be grumbling so. You can remove your great hulking carcass, for it is blocking the entrance to my burrow," replied the ground squirrel.

"I did not mean to block access to your home." I said as I moved my aching body to the side. "Perhaps you could tell me if you have noticed a crow flying about or a mountain lion by the name of Romla?"

"No I haven't seen any crows and I don't converse with mountain lions as a general rule, they tend too readily to eat my kind. Will you please move along? I really can't have strangers loitering about the entrance to my burrow. What are you anyway?"

"I'm a raccoon, and my name is Blinkers," I said. "And what is your name?"

"Oh, I'm usually called Grumblebutt, though my real name is Skitters. Now the two of you move along," he grumbled.

"There are three of us and we intend to stay here until the storm is over and the sun is up," I replied somewhat huffily.

"Have you got another mountain lion tucked in between the two of you? Well, okay, I guess you can stay as long I can get back to my burrow. I would have got home sooner, but for that nasty thunderstorm. What are you doing here anyway, interfering with the lives of the indigenous population?" was his somewhat disjointed response.

I began to recount the long tale of recent events back in the park, until I was interrupted.

"I ain't got time for a novel. How about just giving me the short story version? Oh, and is that Rittiticket a she ground squirrel?" inquired Grumblebutt, who seemed to prefer his nickname.

"No, he isn't," I replied.

"Rats!" muttered Grumblebutt. "Must not be any she ground squirrels within miles of this place."

I recounted a shortened version of our travels ending with the present situation. "So we need to re-cross this stream, and find our companions," I concluded.

"Now maybe, just maybe, I can help you with that. There used to be a rickety old bridge just upstream from here. This flood has probably washed it away, but we could check it out. Most likely it will collapse when you try to cross, but it might not."

As we were talking morning light began to creep into the small cave in which we had sought sanctuary. So I stretched my legs, sniffed the air and warily crept out into the open. Almost immediately Cawdor dropped from the sky to perch on a nearby boulder.

"Anybody else hiding out there with you?" he asked.

"Oh yes, both Pabatackle and Wanda are still in there; we've been conversing with one of the locals."

"Well, that's a relief; we weren't sure what had happened to the three of you. Zornova sent me out as soon as it began to get light to search for signs of you. Now we've got to find a place for you to re-cross this nasty creek. Too bad you weren't bright enough to be born like me, with wings!" he chuckled."

"Yeah, right! Our new acquaintance says that there used to be an old rickety bridge upstream a ways. Could you go and tell Zornova that we're all okay, then go look for that bridge?" I answered.

"That I can do. Bye."

I shouted up after him, "If you see any she golden mantled ground squirrels, let us know? Thanks."

Cawdor had a quizzical expression on his dark features as he glanced back at me before soaring skyward.

As Grumblebutt had suggested, there was indeed a rickety old bridge upstream. We traveled slowly from Grumblebutt's burrow along the stream's edge. Though the water level of the stream was receding, the flow was still powerful. We had to work our way around several newly eroded gullies and rockslides, but eventually we made it to the ramshackle bridge. A number of boards were missing leaving gaps over which we had to jump gingerly. We walked with great care for one of the supports on the far bank looked in danger of collapse. When we moved the bridge creaked and shook ominously. Fortunately the stream was narrow and the bridge was not long. We were soon reunited with Keeble, Romla, Rittiticket, and Zornova, who had viewed our progress across the bridge with some anxiety.

Oh, and before I forget about it, I must tell you that we met Mixiepixie on our way to the bridge. Pabatackle, who was ever curious, stuck his snout into the entrance to her burrow. Mixiepixie, the resident of this burrow, was, as we soon learned, a small she ground squirrel. Grumblebutt was so ecstatic in his hopping and cavorting around that he almost tumbled down a newly eroded rut and into the rushing waters of the stream. As soon as he saw us across the bridge we saw him racing back towards Mixiepixie's burrow, his cheeks all puffed out because they were full of grass seeds for his newly beloved.

We learned that our larger companions had escaped the waters almost without incident. Zornova had slipped on a loose rock and almost fallen into the waters, but had regained her footing in time to avoid a great splash into the stream. After a brief period of reunion we headed west again with Cawdor flying above us. A long mountain ridge that ran from north to south dominated the terrain ahead of us.

"Well, there isn't much out there after this mountain," said Cawdor," after preening his ruffled feathers smooth again. "You have a sandy stretch to cross before you reach a shallow lake. Then you follow a creek upstream from the lake until you reach a spot near the summit of the mountain. There's a gravel road that continues on north, maybe if the moon is bright enough you can travel north then west along that road. Even now there is only an occasional car or truck on that stretch of road."

We crossed the sandy wasteland at night. All of us except Wanda took at least a brief dip in the shallow lake. We followed the dusty, dry bank along that creek up and up. Among the rocks we found a bit a shade where we waited for the cool of evening, before heading up to the summit itself.

From the summit we could see forever, or so it seemed. Cawdor pointed out the sandy waste we had crossed. Ahead of us was a repeat of the terrain we had just crossed, dust and gravel stretching out forever. It was depressing to see how far we had to go. There were big lakes to the north, their waters reflecting the setting sun. But they were surrounded by marshes, not the snowy mountains of the dream that we had all shared. We soon headed down along a gravel road, each of us lost in our own silent thoughts. I was depressed. My feet were sore from crossing the harsh, rocky landscape. None of the others seemed to have any interest in the magnificent scenery that surrounded us. Zornova's head hung low, as though she was burdened by thoughts of bringing all of us into this unknown land searching for answers where none might be found. Keeble was limping slightly; Rittiticket clung to her back to avoid falling off. Dust rose up behind us as we trudged forward following our dream.

For days we trekked onward crossing few roads, and those were unpaved; few humans were to be seen. Near a scattered collection of lakes we saw antelope off in the distance, but they did not approach us. Yet we could not help but remember our friends Zeecor Manata and Cawalla Pan. Even those good memories could not stop the heat from baking us as we traveled or rested during the day. The nights had become colder as summer began to stretch into fall. We did glimpse snowy peaks off to the west, but they always appeared distant, their white slopes glinting in the sun.

We crossed a major highway the next night, careful to avoid the large trucks droning through the night. Slowly the terrain was changing to scattered trees, giving us hope that we would reach the clear lake, and the answers we sought so desperately. Our days and nights were much the same. With more trees to give us cover and shade we made our way more often during the daytime, though one day was fraught with a fearful moment.

I was down by a stream looking for lunch. The water was cold and clear as I scampered in and out of the stream washing the nuts and seeds that I had found. In one area delicious leafy greens grew along the bank. All of a sudden, there erupted a great snaring duel somewhere behind me on the bank. I turned to see Romla and another cougar rolling, biting and clawing furiously at one another. I watched as they alternately lunged and grappled with claws and jaws. Finally Romla bested the other great cat. It slunk away, but turned just before heading up over a slight rise and bid us farewell with a menacing snarl.

I rushed to Romla to see whether or not she was hurt. Her sleek brown coat was clotted with blood in numerous places, where claws and teeth had ripped her skin. I scurried around finding what I needed to attend to her wounds. By now Pabatackle and Zornova, no doubt having heard the growling, had gathered round us.

"This is just dreadful, your beautiful fur all bloody and torn," I muttered as I tended her wounds "Why were you fighting with that other mountain lion? What need was there for a nasty fight and then the cleaning up of messy wounds afterwards?"

"Blinkers, you silly raccoon," panted Romla, "you were about to be that cougar's next meal. He was crouching in the underbrush about ready to spring on you, when I interrupted him!"

"Oh!" I said, stunned almost to silence by this revelation. "Then I owe you my life Romla."

"No, you owe me nothing, you helped rescue Wanda, and you pulled Pabatackle out of that flooded stream. We all help each other, we rescue each other," was Romla's reply.

Soon Zornova, Keeble, Rittiticket, and the others gathered round, having heard the hubbub, and rushed to see what was going on.

Dreaming of the Great Mountains

AFTER ROMLA'S fight we spent the rest of the day taking it easy. Fortunately most of Romla's wounds looked worse than they were. None were very deep. I would need to check them regularly to see that they did not become infected. On the morning following the fighting cougars incident, we ate a late breakfast and began our climb upward towards the great mountains. Some of the tallest peaks were snow covered. Several to the north of us rose high up into the cloudless sky. On the slopes of the mountains that rose up in front of us the trees grew closer together, so we followed trails and old gravel roads when we could, for blazing a trail through the woods was time consuming, because of the fallen trees and areas of rocky scree.

Before dawn the next morning, we crossed over another major highway. Our climb became steeper as the mountains seemed to grow ever taller before us. We were weary from weeks of travel. We spoke little. Even Pabatackle's antics seldom got a laugh anymore. When he popped out on the trail before us with two branched sticks held up to his head like a deer's antlers Keeble merely sighed "yet another goofball routine," and then gently nudged him off the trail and out of the way.

"Bunch of sourpusses, that's what you are," Pabatackle shouted towards our hind ends.

Nobody even bothered to argue with that claim, for we began to doubt the necessity of this trip. What could we find that would help us in this faraway place? And even if we did find anything, would we be able to return in time to do anything to help those whom we had left behind? Finally weary from the day's climb we found a resting place near a small lake just as the moon rose above the trees. We huddled together wordless and despondent. Soon we slept; at least I slept and I assumed the others did too.

It did not take long for me to fall into sleep for I was so very exhausted. My paws, as usual, ached from so much walking. My fur was filthy, covered with spiders' webs, fir needles, and other litter, but I was too tired even to groom myself. I didn't even scurry around looking for a bedtime snack. Then, when I awoke, or at least it seemed like I awoke, I found myself staring across a wide clear reflection of sky. But the lake before me was not the one next to which we slept. Steep cliffs and rocky peaks, very different in size and shape from those around the small lake where we were camped, encircled the lake in my dream, which was surrounded by tall, dark trees. It was then that I noticed my seven companions were with me; they were staring at a small cone-shaped island that rose up out of the sky blue water.

"How do we get to the island?" asked Rittiticket, breaking the silent, windless morning air.

"That may take some doing," answered Zornova, "but I know who can search for a way to get across the lake. Blinkers and Pabatackle, you are the two of us best suited to find a way for us to cross this deep-water lake. Cawdor has flown out over the lake and reported that there is only one place on the lake where there were any boats. These, so it seems, are used to ferry tourists out to the small island and back. So, late in the afternoon, you must scout out the boat landing, once the tourists have gone for the day."

I remember that as the sun sank behind the western rim of cliff and mountains Pabatackle and I began our climb down the steep trail towards the boat landing. Pabatackle had just slid into a rock and knocked his head badly, and I was repeating over and over to myself "Oh how will we ever get across?" when I felt myself being nudged. It was then that I really woke up. Instead of a clear blue sky there was only blackness surrounding me.

"Wake up, Blinkers," Keeble implored me. "Now be careful, back up slowly and everything will be fine."

Without knowing why, I followed Keeble's directions. Soon I was stepping down onto fir needles and dried leaves. "What's going on?" I asked.

"You must have walked in your sleep Blinkers; you were about ready to step off that rock. If you had done so you would have fallen and hurt yourself on the rocks below," Keeble replied calmly.

"But how did you find me in this blackness?" I asked.

"Actually Rittiticket was the one who came and got me. He said that you stepped on him and did not respond when he grumbled at you. Then he followed you up onto that rocky outcrop. When he pulled at your fur and you did not waken, he raced back to fetch me. When I arrived you were moaning 'oh how will we ever get across.' Then it seemed as though you were going to step off the edge, so I decided that I must wake you before you fell and hurt yourself."

"I feel like such a fool, walking about in my sleep and all. I don't think I've ever done that before. Thank you so much Keeble. And now I must find Rittiticket, to thank him too!" I muttered.

When we got back to the circle where we had all been asleep we found everyone awake. Soon we learned, to everyone's amazement, that each of us had slept strangely. Although I was the only one to walk in my sleep, I was not the only one to dream of that lake, so clear and deep. Each of us related to the others what we had dreamt. My story of coming to the lake's shore did not surprise anyone.

Romla related her dream next: "What I remember most vividly is crossing a paved road at night. The rest of you had just got across, and I was bringing up the rear. All of a sudden I was staring into two bright beams of light heading towards me along the roadway. Wanda, who was riding on my back, fluttered to my ear shouting 'move it quick, if you don't want to end up as road kill!' I awakened just as the light, and the roaring noise that accompanied it, bore down upon me. It was indeed a scary dream, much scarier than fighting with a living cougar."

"I don't remember that," said Wanda in her gentle voice. "But I do remember speeding across the surface of the lake in the darkness with the moon and stars bright in the sky above us. I had to crawl inside one of Keeble's ears to keep from being blown away. Keeble so wanted to twitch her ear because my small feet were tickling her, but she remained steadfast and I did not get blown away."

"I don't recall any boat ride," responded Keeble, "but I do remember trying to step down into a boat filled with seats for humans. The boat rocked slightly because Pabatackle was darting from one side to the other to look into the water. Finally, I managed to get down into the boat. Then Zornova, who was waiting behind me, had to figure out how to get carefully into the boat. She was worried that the boat's hull would not hold her weight. Her dread was that she would put her hoof through the hull and that the boat would sink. However, after some careful planning, Zornova was able to step gingerly and softly into the boat."

Zornova spoke next, "I can see how stepping down into a boat might be my concern, but that's not what I remember from my dream. What I remember is seeing Cawdor silhouetted against the moon above as it rode high in the night sky. He was flying lookout for many great logs afloat upon the lake's surface. If we were to run into one of those logs, it would be the end of us all. Once he came swooping down screaming 'turn left, turn left!' as he flapped his wings madly."

Cawdor, with a sardonic cackle, took up the dream story. "Well I may indeed have been flapping my wings wildly and shouting loudly, but that didn't happen in what I remember of my dream. Instead, I remember laughing when Rittititcket sat down on a switch that must be used to turn on the boat's microphone. Then Rittiticket's crabby voice spread across the waters, 'Rats, there ain't no comfortable place for a rodent to sit on this boat. Nobody ever considers what he or she scatters about a surface. My rump's going to be badly bruised before this night is over.' It was then that Rittiticket realized that he was sharing his soft mutterings with everyone on board. He shut up quick and moved off that switch faster than a prairie dog with a hawk on his tail."

"I can't help but think that you made that up Cawdor," grumped Rittiticket. "I am much too dignified to engage in private conversations about my posterior. What I remember is Blinkers trying to steer that dratted boat. The old masked secretary could barely see above that steering doohickey that turns the boat to the right or left. While Blinkers steered Pabatackle moved the throttle lever. All the while Blinkers kept shouting 'slow down your silly otter, you're going to get us all killed.'"

"Hey that sounds like fun," chortled Pabatackle, "and maybe that is going to happen, I surely don't know. What I remember of my dream happened on that cone shaped island. We were all climbing up, over loose rocks, towards the top. But when we got there we found nothing."

"I for one don't like that ending," I said.

"Again we have all dreamed a dream that focuses on our journey. None of us has dreamed or remembered the whole dream. So we don't know if what we dreamt will happen, or whether it is just that we are all concentrating on the fears we have or the weariness we share. What our dreams clearly show us is that our journey still will bring us into harm's way. The way ahead of us will put difficulties in our way that will test us. We must face these difficulties with clear heads and brave hearts. Our dreams also make it clear that all of us have a role to play, that each of us is important if we are to succeed in our quest," concluded Zornova.

At this point we were all awake and faint hints of light were beginning to spread across the night sky. We set about looking for food and cleaning ourselves before again heading towards the steep ascent to the west. Zornova and Keeble grazed near the lake's edge. I waded out into the lake, as I usually do, to wash my food. Pabatackle, after he had dined on fir cone seeds, was frolicking with several members of the local fish community. Wanda flitted around while Rittiticket munched seeds from a fir cone. Romla had disappeared and so had Cawdor as they searched for breakfast. It was a beautiful crisp morning with a clear, blue, sky spreading out above, but it was difficult not to focus on the dreams we had related to one another.

Soon Zornova called for us to gather by the lake's edge. "We have only a short distance to go. Cawdor has seen the reverse outline of the mountains he saw in his dream. Yet the terrain is rugged and we can't be sure that the weather will remain pleasant. Romla, you can scout out the best route for us to take. Cawdor, you continue to lead us from above towards that line of mountain peaks. The rest of us will follow."

As the sun rose in the sky we enjoyed its warmth, for the air was cool and crisp and the sounds of the forest were clear and bright. For a while a pair of gray jays followed our progress through the forest. They sped overhead from one branch to another. We passed a mother elk and her calf. I caught myself missing Tromengard and Udena. How could I miss that irksome moose, I thought? I realized how much I missed Geyser District, my office now burnt and destroyed, and all of my friends back home. My sorrowful mood was soon matched by an incoming weather front. Darker, thicker clouds followed wisps of clouds. As we climbed higher we entered a quieter world of clouds and mists and muffled silence.

Cawdor flew down to join us and perched on Zornova's back just as we reached Romla who was waiting for us to catch up with her.

"It is too thick out there to see anything," said Cawdor. "We are just about to come to the top of a ridge. We want to follow this ridge upward and to the northwest before we drop down and cross a river. It may well be time to camp out overnight when we reach the ridge. We must be careful as we head down that slope for it is steep and there are some cliffs and rock outcropping that should be avoided."

Romla added, "Cawdor is right. We are almost up to the ridge top. The ridge is rocky and uneven with cliffs along the northern slope. I was able to get a brief view of the terrain ahead when the clouds parted for a moment. We will need to follow the south side of the ridge and avoid the top of the ridge."

At that moment Pabatackle shouted with glee! "Put on your skies brothers and sisters; its snow time."

Sure enough snow had begun to fall.

"We must move on, and we must move quickly. Romla, you continue to lead the way. Keeble, you can help lead us too. Cawdor, fly ahead through the trees and do what you can to help us find the easiest path," commanded Zornova with some urgency. "We do not want to get lost in an early snowstorm."

We plodded through the deepening snow, except for Wanda who had burrowed down deeply into the thick fur on Zornova's back. Soon Rittiticket joined her on Zornova's back, when the snow had become too deep for him to clamber through. At least there was no wind so we could hear Cawdor's directions from up above in the trees. Even with Cawdor's help we had to backtrack to get around several obstacles that could not be detected through the falling snow. One time the trail we were following ended in a washout. Then another time we had to retrace our steps when we came to a blow down, a mass of tangled trees that the wind had pushed down several winters ago. Huge trees, with massive trunks, lay scattered before us like so many twigs. There would be no way through this tangle of trunks, branches, and roots.

Eventually, though there were moments of discouragement, we found the ridge and followed it to the northwest. When the ridge ended in a large cliff we dropped down the southern slope until we reached a river. The snow never stopped and our voices were swallowed and softened by the blanket of snow that wrapped us all with its silent persistence. By the time we reached the river we were bone cold and tired, but Zornova did not let us stop to rest. Keeble soon found a log bridge thick and sturdy enough to hold Zornova's weight as she crossed the river. It was also beneath that log and up against a rock overhang that we found a place to camp. Everyone, even Pabatackle, was tired, for he curled up in a ball to sleep rather than frolic in the snow. All of us curled up together in a large mound of fury warmth.

When we awoke the next morning, though it was hard to tell that it was morning deep down in this cove cut by the river, the snow was still falling from low hanging clouds. We roused ourselves, shook off our sleep and peered out into a wall of flakes.

"We must stay here for now," said Zornova wearily. "We do not want to end this journey walking in circles until we are frozen. No one ventures out unless it is to search for food, and even then do not leave our shelter without a partner. In fact we will institute a buddy system. Cawdor and Wanda will be with me. Keeble, you keep Rittiticket and Pabatackle with you. Romla and Blinkers you stay together for now. Get what rest you can, conserve energy, and stay as warm as you can. Blinkers you go with Romla to look for tree boughs to line our refuge so that we need not lie down on the cold ground."

"Certainly, certainly we will find cedar boughs, fir boughs. Oh I'm so sorry to be jabbering on like an idiot, but, but my brain is frozen. So it's not really my fault you see. When one has a frozen brain there's no telling what might issue forth out of the mouth." It was only When I felt a yank on my tail that I realized I had been babbling again. "Well it can't be helped you know. I'm not responsible for the snow am I? Certainly you can't blame me." The second and stronger yank on my tail was finally enough to shut me up.

Romla and I found lots of downed branches and pulled them back to the cavity below the large log and rock overhang. All of us found something to eat before settling into a long day of waiting. The snow slacked off and eventually stopped, but the clouds remained. Night came and we slept.

When we awoke the next morning Cawdor was hopping about on top of us shouting. "Let's get going, the sky is clear and blue and all you have to do is climb up to the top of this ridge. The lake of our dreams is on the other side."

"That's easy for you to say you big cackle-bag," retorted Rittiticket. "You don't have to stomp through snow seven times deeper than you are tall."

"I can't help it if you weren't smart enough to be born with wings," Cawdor spat back in with a saucy tone.

"Okay, okay," growled Romla, "that's enough." At least she was smiling when she spoke, indicating that some good-natured bickering was better than more snow.

Zornova interrupted our silliness, "We do need to get started so let's gather round to plan out our approach to the lake." After we had drawn closer she continued, "Cawdor can give us a report on the nature of the terrain. Then we can decide what needs to be done to get to the boat dock and across the lake to the island. For what we all knew was that we must get to the island, since this is what our dreams all foretold."

"Once over this ridge," Cawdor began "you will soon drop down to a paved road which circles around this side of the lake. On the north side of the lake towards the east is a steep trail leading from the road down to the boat dock. The island is closer to the other side of the lake, in the southwest section. It is shaped like a small volcanic cone. Large machines are clearing snow from the road so you will want to avoid these machines."

Romla spoke next. "Perhaps we should avoid the road?"

"Yes," replied Cawdor, "it might be best if you follow this ridge around to the northeast and cross over once you are closer to the trailhead."

"It would be best for Wanda and me to ride on either Zornova or Keeble's back, since the snow is so deep!" piped up Rittiticket.

"Okay," said Zornova, "this is what we will do. Rittiticket and Wanda will ride on Keeble's back. If we run into deep snow, Blinkers and Pabatackle can ride on my back. We will follow the ridge as Cawdor suggests, staying down low and in the trees at all times. Romla will scout ahead for the best route through the forest. Keeble and I will follow to make a path through the snow for Blinkers and Pabatackle. Cawdor, after you get us started in the right direction, I want you to scout out the island. Once you have checked out the island then fly to the dock and find out as much as you can about the boats. Let's go!"

Romla set out first with Cawdor up above shouting down directions. The rest of us followed along behind. Every so often I had to grab a hold of Pabatackle, to keep him from playing in the snow.

As the morning wore on and the sun ascended higher in the sky, the snow began to soften and melt. We sunk into the soft snow, which made travel more difficult for all of us. Romla would drop back or wait for us every so often to make sure that we took the best route through the trees and around boulders. She did such a good job that we avoided finding ourselves at the top of some steep drop-off with nowhere to go but back the way we had come. By early afternoon Cawdor returned to us.

"You have only a short distance to go before you reach the best place to cross the ridge before you drop down to the highway," he said. "So you should find a place to rest until it is darker and there are no more cars on the road."

"Thanks Cawdor," responded Zornova. "What is the situation at the boat dock?"

"All of the boats are still tied up," replied Cawdor. "It must be because of the snow. They were just finishing plowing the parking area when I came to find out how far you guys had come. Very few cars have been on the road that has been plowed, so you should be able to cross it safely once it gets dark."

We found a good place to rest in the sun just a little further on. The snow had melted enough to allow some strands of grass to pop back up through the soft snow. This pleased both Keeble and Zornova.

"Cawdor, could you tell us more about the boats and the dock?" asked Zornova.

"Well, I don't know how helpful I can be since I don't know much about boats," Cawdor admitted. "But the boats are fairly long, certainly big enough to hold the seven of you. I'm not sure how they are operated. But they are all just alike; all of them are filled with seats for human passengers. Clearly it will be up to Blinkers, Pabatackle, and Rittiticket to operate the boat. Wanda is too small and hooves won't be of much use for operating the controls."

"What is the trail like down to the boats?" Zornova wanted to know.

"It's pretty steep, and there are steps in places, but I don't think they will pose any insurmountable problem," said Cawdor. "How you and Keeble get into a boat and ride in it is probably the more difficult issue."

"So what's the plan?" asked Wanda.

"Well, we know from our dreams that it is Blinkers who steers the boat while Pabatackle mans the throttle," piped up Rittiticket, not wanting to be left out of the planning. "Keeble and Zornova will need to squeeze in between the seats with Zornova near the center of the craft since she is the heaviest. I can perch up on the bow of the boat and watch for rocks and for anything floating in the water while Cawdor flies above making sure we head in the right direction."

"Very well done my little rodent friend, but what do I do?" asked Romla.

"You will need to be the last one aboard," chirruped Rittiticket. "You can hold the rope that is used to secure the boat to the dock in your mouth, and then jump aboard once we are ready to go."

"Very well done, Rittiticket!" I exclaimed. "Very well done indeed!"

"We should all take it easy for now," interrupted Zornova, "For we have a busy night ahead of us and we need to be ready for whatever happens."

So we all settled down as comfortably as possible to sleep.

To the Lake

ZORNOVA PRODDED us awake gently with her hooves. The sun had sunk low in the western sky. Each of us stretched and did our best to leave sleep behind us and prepare for the adventure that lay ahead. I was scared because I knew that I must do something that I had never done before. None of us spoke. It was as though each of us was lost in thought about the task we had before us. Soon we were all gathered and waiting to begin.

Zornova interrupted the silence. "Let's go."

Cawdor flew up into the evening sky. Romla again went first to search out the best rout down to the roadway and then to the trail leading to the dock. Soon the stiffness of my muscles left me as I threaded my way between trees and large stones following behind Zornova. Even Pabatackle seemed to be a in a serious mood. A rare moment indeed!

We could now see the road below us through the trees. As we came to a bare patch of rock Cawdor descended.

"There are no cars on the road," he reported. "If I see any cars or trucks approaching I will signal with three caws. No people are down by the boats either; so far things are looking good."

As Cawdor flew back into a darkening sky we worked our way down toward the road. We walked along the edge of the road, just off the pavement. We had to follow the road for several hundred yards to reach the parking lot and trail on the other side. Just then we heard Cawdor's three piercing caws.

"Scatter!" ordered Zornova, firmly.

Zornova was the only one who faced any real difficulty in finding a place to hide. I found myself, along with Rittitickett, behind a large boulder about twenty feet above the highway. Keeble had bounded quickly across to the other side and then down to a small cluster of wind-stunted trees. Romla covered fifty feet and quickly leaped up onto an overhanging ledge and out of sight. But Zornova stood there as if frozen, not able to see any place to go. I had about decided to go to her when I heard Pabatackle call out.

"Zornova, come here and lie down in this deep ditch!" cried Pabatackle.

But she did not move. It was then that I saw the light from the headlight moving towards her along the road. Pabatackle had to run out and bite Zornova's leg to get her moving. Just as the headlight reached the roadway in front of our hiding place Zornova flopped herself into the ditch. Pabatackle had saved her; kept her from being seen or run into. The large truck moved off loudly around a curve in the road and was gone.

Romla called out, "Let's go!"

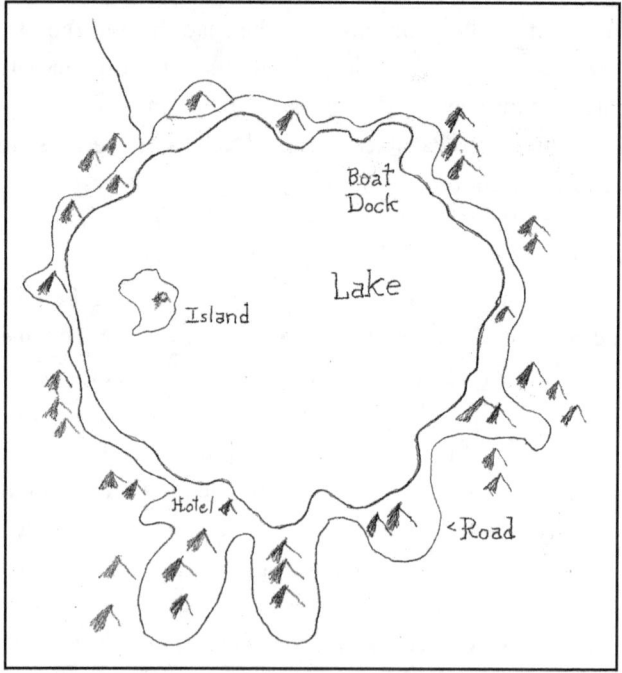

We moved down the road as quickly as possible and soon found ourselves at the trailhead down to the boats. Romla again led the way. Zornova had some trouble with steps that were difficult to see, since it was now almost completely dark. Only a faint and jagged line of light could be seen along the ridge of mountains to the west. Soon we were at the trail's end. Cawdor sat waiting for us perched on a barrier gate across the end of the dock. Pabatackle and I climbed over the gate. Romla and Keeble both leapt easily over the gate. Rittiticket squeezed through the wire fencing. Only Zornova remained on the other side.

Rittiticket scrambled up the gate to examine the latch.

"Well, I bet Blinkers could operate this latch, but blast it all, this gate is securely locked with this padlock," grumbled Rittiticket.

Pabatackle too went to take a look.

"Perhaps you will just need to break down the gate, Zornova?" said Keeble in her calm and even voice.

We all moved down toward the dock, away from the gate. Zornova came closer and examined the barrier. It was all metal and wire mesh. She studied it to find the weakest points. She first backed up a few steps; then lowered her massive head before surging forward towards the gate. The lock did not snap but the gate bent in towards the middle. She backed away again. She rushed forward again. This time when her head crashed into the barrier there was a popping and screeching of breaking metal. The lock snapped and the remains of the gate lurched open on the remaining bottom hinge before clattering onto the deck.

"Let's go boating," muttered Zornova. It was as though this action requiring such strength had re-energized her after her failure of nerve up on the highway. We decided it might be easiest to use the boat closest to the end of the dock. Both Keeble and Zornova had some difficulty getting aboard. Zornova, although she did not wish to damage any property, had to destroy a row of seating in order to have enough space. Keeble just had to be careful not to get her long legs tangled in the framework that held the seats in place. Romla waited patiently as I untied the last rope, the one that moored the boat to the dock.

"Hold this in your mouth Romla, but don't leap aboard until we figure out how to get the motor started," I instructed. "But as soon as the engine starts you should leap aboard so you don't get left behind."

I hopped onboard and worked my way forward to find Rittiticket and Pabatackle examining the various buttons and levers near the steering wheel.

"How do we turn it on?" I asked.

"We're not quite sure, but it looks like we may need a key," answered Rittiticket. He pointed to the slot for a key. "I have an idea; I'll be right back."

Rittiticket scurried to the stern, hopped off onto the dock and ran back towards the shore. Once there he began making the oddest of chirruping sounds. "Cherree, chirrup cherree," squeaked Rittitickett over and over.

Soon we noticed small movements among the stones on the shore. The movements turned into a dozen or so ground squirrels. We could hear some talking, but we were too far away to understand the words that were being spoken. The ground squirrels scattered and then came back after fifteen to twenty minutes of searching. Rittiticket headed our way with a doleful countenance. Undoubtedly his idea had not met with success. Later we would find out that this squad of ground squirrels had searched, unsuccessfully, for the key we needed. What would we do now?

All of us except Keeble and Zornova climbed out of the boat and split up searching for the key that was needed to start the boat. After more than an hour of searching we decided we had best head back to safety so that we could re-think our plans. The major difficulty was getting Zornova out of the boat. She accidentally destroyed several more seats as she backed up and then climbed back onto the dock.

"We have a problem," asserted Wanda. "Our nocturnal escapade will not go unnoticed by the people who operate these boats. We need to do a thorough job of disguising our presence here."

"Wanda is right," responded Zornova. "Keeble and I will go hide out on the other side of the road. The rest of you must destroy our hoof prints and clean obvious animal signs from the boat. We can't do anything about fixing the seats in the boat or the broken gate."

Wanda searched the boat for animal prints and Pabatackle washed them away. Romla and I used evergreen boughs to sweep away hoof marks along the trail. It took us several more hours to complete our sweeping job. It was almost daylight when we crossed the road to look for Keeble and Zornova. We were all incredibly discouraged. We had come so far and now we didn't know how to get any further. We trudged several hundred yards away from the road to a wooded area to wait and regroup.

A Second Attempt

L ATE THE next afternoon, after sleeping through the morning and then searching for food, Zornova sent Cawdor and Wanda back to the boat dock to find out what the humans were doing. Soon Cawdor returned.

"Well, there is a great deal of commotion at the site. There are police cars and people with cameras searching about trying to discover who broke the gate and vandalized the boat," reported Cawdor. "Wanda is perched on one of the flasher lights of one of the police cars so she can listen to the radio conversations."

"Oh I do hope she is safe," I exclaimed. "We must be careful not to be seen. We must stay hidden among the trees."

Just as I finished my admonition the loud thrum of a helicopter engine could be heard. Soon a low flying copter passed above us moving towards the parking lot.

After the copter passed and then landed in the parking lot, Zornova spoke softly, "Cawdor, you fly back and observe what is happening. After nightfall we must find another place to wait; we need to be further away from the road. Romla, as soon as its dusk you will search for a better shelter on the far side of the ridge. We may need to wait for several days for another attempt. I want all of you to think about how we might get a key for the boat."

"I have an idea, Zornova," volunteered Rittiticket. "Maybe Cawdor could search for buildings where the key might be kept. Maybe the local ground squirrels would be willing to help us too. Once we know where the key is, Blinkers and I could go try to borrow it. Blinkers has very nimble paws and so do I; between the two of us I'm pretty sure we could eventually find the key we need."

A Second Attempt

"Oh that's too dangerous; it's like looking for a fir cone seed in a sand dune," I replied.

"It won't be easy, but it may be the best plan available to us now," interjected Zornova. "After Cawdor scouts out the boat dock once more the three of you can begin your search for the key."

"I will see if I can get any help from the indigenous rodent population," said Rittiticket. "I've seen several ground squirrels scampering about not too far away; maybe they will help us." He darted off to in search of a ground squirrel who might help.

Cawdor returned to report that most of the police and park vehicles had departed and that Wanda would be back soon. "Tomorrow I will fly south to the hotel and speak to some of the local crows. Maybe they will know something."

Somewhat later Wanda returned as well. "From my perch on the police car," she said, "I could hear that nobody had a clue about what happened on the boat, or who was responsible for the damage. It is clear that they are baffled. Much of the talk centered on human pranksters. They have put yellow plastic bands up all over the place warning people to keep out. Tomorrow the gate is to be repaired."

As Wanda was finishing her story Rittiticket returned with a golden mantled ground squirrel. "This is Funduster," Rittiticket announced, "She has some information that might be useful for us."

"I might be able to help," responded Funduster, somewhat shyly, "for I have been to the great hotel to the south. Near the hotel are other smaller buildings, storage sheds, offices, and other such places. I got there sort of by accident. One day when I was begging for food at the parking lot above the boat dock, I climbed up into the back of one of the green pickup trucks. Before I knew what was happening, the vehicle shuddered, as its motor roared. I crouched down in a corner behind the truck's cab to keep out of the wind. It was very frightening, but I survived. Eventually the truck stopped and I scampered down to the ground. I was surrounded by cars and trucks parked near a large building. I knew this was not a safe place for a ground squirrel. One false move and some car or truck would flatten me into just one more squirrel pancake.

"But to get to the point," Funduster continued, "I'd be happy to help you search the buildings. I did see a large board with lots of keys hanging on hooks. Maybe the key you need is there?"

"I think we should get started tonight," said Rittiticket.

"How can we do that?" asked Wanda.

"Keeble, Blinkers, Cawdor and I will go with Funduster to the great hotel to the south. We will search for the keys that make the boat work. Cawdor will help us get to the hotel. Funduster and I will ride on Keeble's back. We need Blinkers to help search for the keys, since he is our best reader. Won't that work?" said Rittiticket.

"It's the best plan we've got," replied Zornova. "As soon as it's dark you will do what Rittiticket has outlined. The rest of us will remain here out of sight."

None of us was excited about more trekking along roads in the dark, but nobody came up with a better plan. All too soon it was dark and the traffic thinned out. Rittiticket and Funduster climbed up onto Keeble's back. Cawdor flew ahead to scout out the road. We traveled cautiously, staying in the trees whenever that was possible. Just as the sunlight hovered on the horizon Cawdor flew back down.

"We are almost to the hotel. Keeble, there are some trees up ahead, you can hide there while the rest of us go on to the hotel," Cawdor explained.

I had to be especially careful as we snuck between the buildings near the hotel, since I was more noticeable than a ground squirrel. We poked around looking for open doors and windows.

"I think the building with all the keys on a board is over this way," whispered Funduster.

We followed her to a building with several large doors for cars to enter. These doors were still closed. She motioned for Rittiticket to follow her up a drainpipe to a window while I hid behind a nearby rhododendron bush. Soon Rittiticket returned.

"This is the place with the keys," he whispered. "Will you try to open the door?"

I wasn't quite able to reach the doorknob while standing on my hind legs. So we looked for something for me to stand on. After some searching we found a plastic bucket. I had placed it below the knob and had just stood up on the bucket and I was reaching for the doorknob. What happened next about scared me out of my skin.

"Would you look at that, Jenny, that raccoon's trying to open the door," squeaked an excited female voice. "Skedaddle, you pesky raccoon; go on, get out of here."

I got out as quickly as I could. I ran to the other side of the building and hid behind a woodpile.

Soon I heard Rittiticket's giggle. "Yep Funduster, he's still got his skin on. I never saw you move so fast Blinkers," he chuckled.

"I'll go keep watch," said Funduster, barely containing her excitement. "Maybe they will leave a door or window open so we can get inside."

Finally, after the sun crept over the mountains, then rose high, a window was opened to let in some air. Eventually both Jenny and her companion left the building after talking on the phone and filling out some paperwork on a small desk. I followed Rittiticket through the window while Funduster kept watch from the windowsill.

I scanned the top rows while Rittiticket scanned the bottom rows looking for tags that seemed to be for the boats.

"Hey Blinkers, check this one," whispered Rittiticket.

I read the tag, which had the words "boat dock" scrawled on it. "I think that one goes to the padlock on the gate," I suggested. "You might want to bring that along."

I returned to the third row from the top. I saw a tag that read "tour boats." At that moment the door opened; I stumbled and fell from the table. Rittiticket dove from the desk to the floor and skittered behind another desk.

"What the heck is going on here!" yelled a deep-voiced man.

"They were here earlier," answered Jenny's friend.

The man had picked up a broom by then and was headed in my direction. I had the amazing presence of mind to leap up on the desk, grab the boat keys from the rack, and dive through the open window. Though I was just about scared out of my fur, I headed back in the direction of Keeble's hiding place among the trees. I knew that Rittiticket and Funduster could take care of themselves. I managed to get away from the hotel and parking lot quickly. I tried my best to stay behind boulders and shrubs until I was no longer visible from the hotel.

By the time I reached Keeble's refuge I was a bit more in control, though I was still shaking.

"Are you all right Blinkers?" she asked soothingly. Clearly, she wanted to calm me down; I wanted to calm down.

"Yes, I guess so. We almost got caught," I responded.

"Where are Rittiticket and Funduster?" she continued.

Fortunately Cawdor hopped down from one of the lower branches to answer Keeble's second question. "They're on their way here. They are trying not to draw attention like a certain hair-brained raccoon just did."

"I, I'm so sorry," I responded sheepishly.

"Actually, I don't think that more than one or two people saw you, and they probably didn't notice the key ring in your mouth," offered Cawdor consolingly.

Soon Rittiticket and Funduster appeared with another key. We checked the tags; we had got the keys we needed, as far as we could tell. Unfortunately there was not much we could do but wait, except for Cawdor. He flew back to tell Zornova and the others. After calming down, and snacking on fir-cone seeds, we took naps in preparation for our nighttime return.

We made it back to where Zornova, Romla, Pabatackle, and Wanda waited for us without incident.

We were concerned that some bright human might put two and two together and notice that the missing keys were for the boats. They might just think that our theft had something to do with the damaged boat escapade that had occurred so recently. Our concern was unnecessary. Humans, as usual, did not come to the obvious conclusion. At times it is valuable to be perceived as dumb animals.

Once again we repeated our trek down to the boat dock, as we had several days before. We knew that there was no guard posted because Cawdor had scouted ahead for us. Soon we were all aboard another boat, another boat which would need to have some of its seats replaced. I was again at the steering wheel

"Okay, let's try these," gasped Rittiticket, as he dropped a bunch of keys on the seat next to me.

One by one I tried to fit the keys into the slot. After attempting unsuccessfully to shove six keys into the slot the seventh slipped easily into place. I turned the key and the engine sputtered then stopped. I pushed a lever, turned the key again, and the engine roared to life. I felt the reverberation of Romla's feet landing in the boat.

"Pabatackle, try pushing this lever slowly. Maybe that will get us moving, I ordered. It didn't. But several levers later we started to move forward. Cawdor, who had been patiently waiting in front of the glass windscreen, surged into the sky. Every so often he would let out a "caw" and I would steer toward it. Rittiticket scurried up to the very front of the bow to act as lookout. We moved, actually lurched, forward slowly, until Pabatackle figured out how to work the throttle.

"Turn left, turn left!" shouted Rittiticket.

I turned left. We barely missed hitting a log floating on the surface. After that Cawdor stayed a little closer to us, circling just a few yards above lake's surface. I could see nothing; it was like steering through ink, totally black. All of us had realized too that our boat ride would not go undetected for very long; the roar of the motor bounced noisily off the wall of cliffs surrounding the lake. Later I found out that Romla had seen cars moving along the road towards the boat dock. But I was too frightened and too busy trying to steer the boat to notice anything.

Just then Cawdor flapped down onto the bow.

"We are almost there," he shouted above the noise of the motor. "It will be tricky landing at the dock!"

Landing at a dock! I don't know anything about landing a boat at a dock. My stomach muscles began to tighten, as I grew more scared.

"Pabatackle, we must land very slowly!" I cried.

"When we get closer I will turn the engine off so we can float towards the dock," he answered, sounding calm and assured.

"I can see the dock!" squeaked Rittiticket.

Pabatackle cut the engine. Slowly we glided through the inky darkness towards the dock. As we came softly along side, Romla bounded out of the boat with the rope in her mouth. Soon Pabatackle was out of the boat helping to tie the mooring ropes to small stanchions. I sat there frozen, unable to move.

"Blinkers!" hissed Rittiticket from the dock.

I became aware of eyes staring at me. Wanda hovered nearby, her small wings beating the air, creating a soft buzzing sound on the now quiet air above the lake. "Yep, I think he's turned into a statue," she giggled. She landed on my nose, tickling it, causing me to sneeze. "Come on now," she whispered.

Somewhat sheepishly I followed the others along the dock.

We knew where we had to go. We worked our way among the rough boulders that lay strewn about the ground. Cawdor flew above and Romla led the way. There was a trail, but in the inky blackness of the night it was easy to stumble off to the side. It did not take us too long to get to the top of the cinder cone, the highest point of the island.

"So what do we do now?" asked Pabatackle.

"We don't know," answered Keeble, "for none of our dreams included this part of our search for an answer. Maybe we need to be quiet and wait."

"Yes," said Zornova, "we will be quiet and wait."

For a while we mostly noticed each other's breathing. Soon the darkness surrounded us completely; it was almost as though it entered us. I became frightened by the darkness, the emptiness of the night on the barren island where there seemed to be no life.

The Answer

AFTER WHAT seemed like an eternity of silence we heard a small voice speak. "So you have come. I have been waiting, but I was not sure you would make it this far."

"So you know who we are and where we are from?" asked Zornova softly.

"Yes and no," the voice responded. "I know that you have traveled far, for the winds' voices have whispered tales of your journey into my ears. I know that you have come from the east, but the voices are sometimes vague."

"Do you know why we have come?" was Zornova's response.

"Like the others you seek an answer," the voice replied. "I will tell you two things. First, although this lake is deep and clear, it is not the place where all is made clear. You must look deep inside yourselves and search the spirit within you, if it is clarity you desire. And, secondly, I will tell you that the answer is also to be found in your journey. For even though the answer you seek is held within your hearts, you would not have believed the answer without this journey. That is all that I can really tell you that will help to you."

"Who are you? Do you have a name?" asked Wanda. "We are so tired and we have come so far from home, we would at least like to know who it is that gives us this answer."

"I am Arachanar, a weary and ancient spider who should have died; a spider who wishes she would have died decades ago. But I do not die like all of the other spiders. I weave my webs between the boulders and catch the voices of the wind. They speak to me of many things. The voices tell me of flames and great suffering in the east. They tell me too of beauties I shall never see with my own eyes. You are not the first to come to me with questions, nor will you be the last, but you are among the bravest, for you have journeyed farther than most."

"Thank you for your answer," sighed Zornova wearily. "We will need to ponder it if we are to understand its meaning. Is there anything you want from us in return for your answer?"

"No," answered Arachanar, "the winds provide all that I need, except death. And death will come when another is ready to take my place. I will tell you two more things. Beware of the dogs tainted by humans, for they are watchful. Their numbers have increased and they wait for your return, hoping that this time they will destroy you. Further, I admonish you to choose the way of peace, for violence will not help you nor the ones who await your return. Hurry on your way, all of you, for the humans will soon come to search for the boat you have taken. Farewell."

"Farewell, Arachanar," was Zornova's reply.

Somewhat dejected and confused by Arachanar's answer we turned and moved carefully down the trail towards the boat dock. Moments after we began our descent the roar of a boat motor rent the silence of the lake. Now the humans were after us too. How would we escape from them when the only way back up from the lake was the trail beyond the boat dock, where other humans waited while still more humans pursued us on the water? We were exhausted from our long journey, how would we be able to make our escape and return to our home in the Geyser District? And what good was the answer we had been given for all those who awaited our return? There was no time for reflection now. Now was the time for action!

"Carefully now," instructed Zornova, "we must keep our minds sharp if we are to survive. First we must return to the main boat dock on the shore by an irregular route. Station yourselves as you did on the way here."

We all scrambled to our places. Well, Zornova and Keeble did not scramble, but they were soon aboard and ready to go.

Pabatackle and I got the motor going and Romla jumped aboard quickly. We started out by circling to the other side of the island where we could not be easily found by the other boat. The other boat had been moving towards the island as we cast off. We heard the other boat's engines slow as it approached the island.

"Go!" cried Zornova, "go as fast as we can!"

Pabatackle pushed the throttle lever and we sped forward. Cawdor flew just ahead of us. Rittiticket tumbled back towards the windscreen, blown off his feet by the wind. He skittered around the windscreen and sat down.

"Ouch, this boat surely isn't designed for the comfort of rodents," his voice surged loudly across the lake. He must have turned on some microphone device. We all remained quiet while Rittiticket fidgeted, pushing buttons and switches. Before long a small red light went out.

I whispered, "Are we quiet now?" Apparently the microphone was turned off again. "Zornova," I almost shouted, "maybe we can confuse the humans on the main dock by giving them confusing messages."

"Yes, yes!" Rittiticket agreed. "We could tell them that the runaway boat has been damaged, and is about to sink, but that it appears to be abandoned. We could say we need help to search the waters for the survivors who must have jumped off."

"Yes, we must form a plan," whispered Keeble in her calm voice.

"But we are not allowed to speak to humans," I interjected.

"Blinkers, the plan is to make them think we are humans. The biggest problem is, what do we say, and which of us has the voice that could fool the humans long enough for us to get past them," Keeble reminded us.

We needed to make up our minds about what to do before the first boat reached us. We did not have the time to formulate some elaborate plan. "Pabatackle you must jump out and thrash about in the water as though you are a human who has fallen in.

As they come close you must dive and then swim off under water. Once you are far enough away, rise to the surface again and thrash about. But make sure that you keep the humans positioned so they can't be seen from the main dock, the one we started from," I ordered. "The rest of us will head for the main boat dock. Romla will speak into the microphone; she will tell the people to board another boat and follow us quickly to where people have fallen or jumped into the lake on the other side of the island. Once they are racing towards the island we will tell them we must turn back because we will soon run out of fuel. Then we will turn about and race for the dock. Rittiticket will have to operate the throttle. I'm sorry Pabatackle, but you will need to get out of the lake and return to us as best you can. We will send Cawdor to find you as soon as we are well hidden again, on beyond the roadway and ridge line."

"Yes, it is a good plan!" interrupted Zornova. "Jump now."

Pabatackle splashed into the water just as the boat pursuing us came into view. I stayed up steering the boat while the rest of our crew dropped down onto the deck as best they could. Rittiticket took over control of the throttle. Meanwhile, Pabatackle was acting his part well thrashing the surface of the water in a very visible way. Our pursuers slowed to pull him out. He dove under and came up fifty feet away in the opposite direction and repeated his performance of the drowning human. As we raced towards the main dock Romla moved up beside me.

"Rittiticket, you get up here and push the button for me," said Romla.

As we approached the main dock Romla spoke into the microphone: "Man overboard on the other side of Devil's Island. Come quickly. We will head back to attempt a rescue. There may be several people in the water. I repeat—there may be several people in the water."

I turned the boat and headed in the opposite direction, but slowed as if to allow the humans clustered on the dock to jump into another boat and follow us. This is what they did, or at least this is what all but two of them did. Soon the other boat was catching up with us.

Romla spoke again, "We must turn back, our fuel is almost gone. We will refuel and return to help with the search. Good luck!"

With that we turned and raced again for the dock.

"I'm going to come in fast. Cawdor, you fly at the humans and distract them as we approach the dock. As soon as Romla and I have the boat tied to the dock the rest of you must get out as quickly as possible. Rittiticket, you climb up on Keeble, if you think it sounds like a good plan, I mean," as I realized I was ordering everyone about.

"Do it!" ordered Zornova, from the several rows back.

Cawdor flew at the two men from the landward end of the dock, flapping his wings rapidly and cawing loudly as they both turned. They waved their arms. One man dropped what looked like a shotgun into the water. The boat came in a bit fast, hitting the dock with a resounding thump. Romla was out first, and I jumped out almost as quickly. I tied up the boat. Keeble, with Rittiticket on her back bounded onto the dock just as the two men swung about. Both jumped onto other boats tied to the dock, just to get out of her way. Zornova had a bit more difficulty, but managed to clamber up onto the dock with Wanda clinging to her left ear. As we reached the shore Romla turned around and growled in a threatening manner. Both men looked completely dumbfounded.

Soon we were back up at the trailhead. We raced across the parking lot to the roadway. We raced up and over the ridgeline just moments before a car with lights flashing sped by. Cawdor headed out over the lake again to find Pabatackle. We were almost giddy with delight as we realized that we had tricked the humans and managed to get to the island and back. However, our glee subsided as we realized it might be much more difficult for Pabatackle to get back to us. We had had a fast boat, but he had to swim and then find some alternative path back up to the roadway. It was then that we remembered the strange and unclear words spoken to us by Arachanar the spider.

Moments later our calm was again interrupted. A helicopter swooped down and landed in the parking lot. We scrambled down the ridge as quickly as we could, with Romla in the lead. We headed for a dense clump of trees, pushed our way through a tangle of branches and trunks until we found a safe hiding place. For the rest of the night we could hear the noise of vehicles on the road and the helicopter in the sky. As the sun began to creep up into the dark sky to the east Cawdor flapped down to our hiding place.

"Zornova! Keeble! Blinkers!" He called out.

"Yes, Cawdor you have found us," answered Zornova. "Can you tell us where Pabatackle is?"

Cawdor hopped from branch to branch until he entered the dark shade of our hiding place. "Pabatackle is fine. Blinkers, your plan worked just as we had hoped it would. Pabatackle will try to return to us tonight. But since the boats and a helicopter are still searching the lake, he will have to wait until tonight, before risking swimming the rest of the way back. For now he is safely hidden in a cavity beneath a pile of rocks on the southeast shore of the lake, well away from the island and the waters the humans are now searching. One of you will need to come with me down to the dock tonight when it is dark again, in case he needs help."

"Thanks Cawdor, perhaps you should rest for a while. None of us slept well last night with all of the excitement and commotion, so all of us should rest," ordered Zornova.

Back to the Lake before Heading East

LIKE MOST of the rest of our group I had found a comfortable place to sleep. But now something or someone was prodding me. "Who's poking me?" I sputtered.

"It is I, your black-feathered friend," answered Cawdor. "Zornova says you are to come with me to fetch Pabatackle. I've just returned from a surveillance run; the humans have left the boats and the helicopter disappeared several hours ago. Zornova thinks you will have the easiest time getting down to the dock and helping Pabatackle."

"Great, lucky me," I whined. I rubbed the sleep from my eyes and stumbled through the trees and out into the open. Even though I had slept all day my muscles were stiff and my head felt fuzzy. Nonetheless, I snuck back up to the ridge top. Cawdor signaled from above that the road was clear, so I scurried across. Hugging the boulders and tall grass I scurried, as quickly as I could, towards the parking lot. It was too early to go down to the dock, so I found a place to hide near the trailhead on the far side of the parking area. Cawdor flew off to see how Pabatackle was doing. I was so tired I could not stay awake.

Soon, but in reality three hours later, Cawdor was back prodding me with his beak again. "Pabatackle will be back soon. But, whoa, hold your bison, we've got company," he said.

I peered up over the stone outcrop I had hidden behind. Sure enough there was a man leaning against his car looking the other direction, towards the parking lot entrance. But, worse than that, the man had a dog with him. I don't know what brand of dog it was;

it was one of those shorthaired floppy-eared beasts. All I knew was that Cawdor was right; we had a problem.

"We need a diversion big enough to get those two out of the way for a good while," I whispered.

"I'll go get Romla," croaked Cawdor softly. "I'll bet she can create a diversion."

Cawdor flew up into the darkness. I pressed myself against the rock, attempting to become smaller. Although it seemed like an hour or so, Cawdor returned about ten minutes later. Not long after Cawdor's return the dog started howling. I heard Romla let out a great screeching cry in the darkness. It spooked me, and it must have spooked the man. I peeked over the rock outcrop just in time to see the dog bolting across the parking lot. The man, muttering, ran after the dog, at the same time calling after him, ordering him to come back. The dog was too busy running and howling to pay any attention.

I headed for the trail and rushed down to the dock as fast as I could. It was several hundred feet down from the parking lot. Just as I reached the dock I heard a sassy, smarmy voice. "Well it's about time," sneered Pabatackle. "Did you bring food? I'm starved."

"No, you foolish otter," I hissed. "We've got trouble!"

"Do tell, do tell," tittered Pabatackle.

"We need to get out of here quickly and quietly," I whispered. "A man and a dog were guarding the parking lot, and I don't know how long Romla can keep them diverted."

As soon as I mentioned the dog I was pretty sure that Pabatackle would be ready to go, for some time back Pabatackle had had an unfortunate run in with a tourist's Chihuahua. The Chihuahua, named Fifi, had bested our brave and silly otter. Pabatackle's encounter with Fifi had ended unsatisfactorily for Pabatackle. His hind legs had sustained several painful nips. So we climbed up the steps quietly and quickly while Cawdor flew up to check on the parking lot.

Fortunately Romla had successfully diverted the man and his dog, so we fled back along the road, over the ridge and into our shelter in the trees. We both sat there panting, tired out from our hurried run back to safety.

"You two may rest for a bit, but then we've got to move on," announced Zornova. "Romla will return soon, so we must be ready to put some distance between us and those who may want to hunt us. We can't be sure that we will be followed, but we can't be sure that we won't. Cawdor, you fly ahead; be particularly on the lookout for humans with hunting dogs."

Sure enough Romla came quietly back to the hiding place. After a few minutes more of rest, Romla led us towards the southeast and down into the forest below. We knew that we must not dawdle. Early snowstorms could catch us at anytime, and we must get back home before winter started. And, somehow, we must figure out what to do with Arachanar's enigmatic answers to our questions. It seemed so unfair that we were left with merely another riddle to unravel after such a long and dangerous trek across unfamiliar territory.

Our return journey was long, and much of it was tedious. Our attention was on placing one foot in front of another in what seemed like an endless succession. We crossed the long dry mountain ridge on a blustery day. Snowflakes dangled above us in the crisp, sun-less air. A light dusting of snow helped brighten even the darkness of night, making it easier for Cawdor to guide us by the quickest route.

As we approached the great river we found Wickla Ban and Suirica Poul, two antelope, waiting for us. They were grazing contentedly down near the valley floor next to a small stream, about five miles away from the bridge we would re-cross. As soon as we topped a small rise they ambled our way.

"Welcome weary travelers, we have been waiting for you," said Wickla Ban, the elder of the two antelope. "We hope your journey has proved successful. Since it is early afternoon we will rest here for several hours before working our way towards the bridge. Suirica Poul, let the others know that the travelers have returned."

"We are well, but we are tired, so we will take advantage of the rest you have suggested," answered Zornova. "Thank you for your welcome, and thank you for your faithful waiting."

We drank from the stream. Soon Pabatackle was frolicking in the shallow water. Wanda, who was nearing the end of her brief moth's life, perched on a large stone outcrop while I brought her some water. Every day she grew weaker. It was our hope that she would make it back home before she died of old age. Before long all of us were snoozing in the afternoon sun.

Each of us was gently prodded by one of the dozen or so antelope who were there as an escort. Several more would join us as we approached the bridge. By the time the sun was sinking behind the dark silhouette of distant mountains we had reached a point close to the bridge. We would wait here until late in the night when there was no more car and truck traffic. There was very little traffic on this late autumn evening, so we were soon across the river and heading east to a safe resting place for what remained of the night.

When I awoke the next morning and rubbed the sleep from my eyes I saw Zornova conversing with two antelope as short distance away. After stretching I moved slowly towards Zornova and the two antelope. As I got closer I recognized Cawalla Pan and Zeecor Manata. I hurried forward to greet them both.

"Good morning, Blinkers," greeted Zeecor, and then Cawalla.

"It's great to see you again," I replied. "Have you got a good route mapped out for us to follow on our way home?"

"The way home looks good, Blinkers, except for one challenge we must face," answered Zornova. "We must really have angered those dogs we met on our way west, for now there are almost a hundred of them searching for us. But I think I have a plan to get the better of the dogs. We will discuss the plan later, for now we must be on our way."

Rittiticket had just scurried up carefully with Wanda on his back. "Good morning, good morning to all," he chirruped. "I will look after Wanda on the way home, for she is very tired. Who do I ride today?"

Keeble lowered her head to the ground allowing Rittiticket, with Wanda, to surge aboard. Pabatackle and I clamored aboard Zornova, so that we could make better time. When the way got too rough or steep we would get off and follow Zornova until we were back in the wide-open spaces. We traveled this way for two days, covering a good bit of ground. And so far, we had seen nothing of the dogs that sought to hinder us.

The Sacrifice

AFTER ANOTHER night huddled against the cold air we awoke rested and ready to continue on our journey homeward. As we were stretching, looking for food, and slowly waking to this new day a lone antelope approached. This antelope, Phanapee Sto approached Cawalla Pan and Zeecor Manata. Phanapee was limping slightly. The three of them approached us.

"The news is not good," Zeecor began, "all along the way the dogs wait for us. Phanapee escaped to warn us but Zepa Freneck and Delio Canata were brought down by the dogs and destroyed."

"Well then, it looks like we must follow my plan," answered Zornova. "I had hoped to avoid it, but it looks as though we have no real alternative now. We will split into two groups. Keeble, Blinkers, Rittiticket, Pabatackle, Wanda, and Cawdor will follow the ravine to the south while Romla and I head north with the antelope towards where the dogs are waiting. We will be the decoys to divert the dogs and draw their attention away, so that the rest of you may pass unharmed."

"I see what you mean," interjected Keeble, "but I must go with you and Romla. The small ones may sneak past, but I will just call attention to them, for I cannot hide among the rocks or crawl through culverts to safety."

"Yes Keeble, you are right," replied Zornova. "But you must go with the antelope when I command you to do so."

"Yes Zornova," answered Keeble "I will obey you if I can."

"I don't like this plan," interrupted Pabatackle. "It's all wrong, for we are in this together."

"We are in this together," Romla agreed. "And that is why you must get through; that is why you must return to Geyser District, to save the suffering ones that remained behind while we traveled towards the deep lake."

"But we have no answer!" whined Rittiticket. "We have found out nothing on this long trek."

"We have found out everything," answered Zornova "We have found out that our salvation lies in working together, no matter the circumstances. We have found out that we must seek for answers, but that the real answers are within us. We have found out that we must make sacrifices, even though they are painful. We have found out that loving and caring for each other is what is needed more than anything else. We have found out that being willing to look for the answers, no matter the hardship, is the answer itself. And further, we have learned that we are not alone. The great power of the earth and sky has sent us friends to give us strength on this journey. But now it is time to get on with what must be done."

"Though you are right in what you say, Zornova," I put in, "I fear for you and Romla and Keeble, and I worry that the rest of us will not be able to continue our journey without you. Please don't take any risks that are unneeded!"

We said our farewells then headed our separate ways. To obscure this separation a large herd of antelope milled about creating confusion and a large cloud of obscuring dust. Our dispirited group went south, then angled slowly back northeastward. We hid behind outcroppings, scurried through ditches, culverts, and gullies to avoid the patrolling dogs. Zornova, Romla, and Keeble, surrounded by antelope headed north towards the waiting army of dogs.

We eventually realized that we traveled parallel routes. Zornova and the others followed the floor of the valley, drawing the dogs towards them. We circled around and traveled above, along the ridgeline. We met no dogs, for they were all drawn towards the commotion on the valley floor; the ruse had worked as it was intended. But we still worried. And our worries were well founded, for soon the herd of antelope moved closer towards a wall of waiting dogs.

"Cawdor," I said, "you must fly down and observe what is happening below. We will move along the ridge and meet you at the pinnacle ahead of us. Pay close attention so that when you return to us you can tell us all that happens."

Cawdor flew off and we scurried towards the pinnacle, staying to the east of the ridge top so that we might remain undetected. Every so often we would ascend to the ridge top and peer over. It was not long until we could see that the antelope would soon confront the dogs. The antelope, Zonorva, Keeble, and Romla were barely visible and dust rose into the air further obstructing our view. What we could see was that the antelope met the dogs near a large and ancient tree. Nothing happened for a while. Zornova stood still as the dogs attacked her. The dust from their motions rose up and erased our view so that we could no longer tell what was happening. But what we had seen did nothing to hearten us as we plodded onward. The next morning we continued on our way. It was all we could do to take one step at a time, through the cold air that now surrounded us. Soon we met a disheveled and despondent Cawdor at the pinnacle. None of us had the heart to ask Cawdor to tell us what he had witnessed below. But finally I said, "We must know what happened."

Cawdor, gripped tightly by pain, could barely speak. But he forced himself to open his beak and force the necessary words through it. "I arrived at the tree just as the antelope approached the line of dogs, close to a hundred of them. Then Razor, leader of the dogs growled and snarled angrily, 'You will die, all of you will die!' Zornova replied quietly 'You know that if we were to fight you that many of you would die. Remember the sharp hooves of the antelope and Romla the mountain lion's teeth and claws, and I could trample unto death many of you. I could split you open with my horns and spill your entrails across this bowl of rock and dust, but what a waste that would be. I have no desire to see my friends die to save me, nor do I wish to spill your blood either. So I offer myself to you. Rip me to shreds as you please.'"

"Razor snapped and barked, then spoke," Cawdor continued, "'How noble you are, how generous of you to die for your friends, but what if we do not accept your offer?' 'Then we will fight you, and many will needlessly die, if that is what you want,' answered Zornova. Razor ambled back and huddled with other top dogs. I could overhear some of what they said. 'I say we should kill them all,' snarled the old and grizzled Bengor. 'But look you at the size of that bison; remember how she tossed our kin over her back as if they were nothing. See you the mountain lion perched in the tree above; remember her jaws and claws. The antelope too are skilled fighters. See you any fear in their eyes?' asked Razor. Others, lusting after blood and revenge, called out 'Fight them, kill them, and devour them!' But a scarred and wizened female, Jaranzac, interrupted them. 'Do not be fools! Accept the offer, get your revenge, get your blood, devour the bison, but do not lead us into death! A battle would be stupid; this offer will be costly enough.' Razor strutted away from the huddle and approached Zornova."

" 'Though I would have chosen a great battle, and many others thought a battle to be the best choice, we have decided to accept your offer,' answered the puffed up Razor. 'This is how we will proceed,' said Zornova, 'the antelope will back away and you can attack me when you are ready, there are no other rules. I would ask you to promise not to hunt down and harm my companions, for there is no point in that.' Zornova then turned to the antelope and Keeble. 'Go now.' Romla responded, 'I will stay in the tree and I will not interfere.' The antelope moved away and the dogs began to circle warily."

"It soon became clear that Zornova did not intend to attack them. Finally Bengor lunged and bit Zornova from behind, Razor followed snapping and biting. Then other dogs joined in biting, gripping her flesh with their jaws and pulling. Even though it left their lust for revenge unsatisfied, they continued their attack until Zornova, bloody and weary, toppled to the ground. Some continued to attack and rip her with their jaws, but there was no satisfaction in it for them. Soon, one by one, they began to slink away, until none were left. I flew down to check on her, but there was no doubt that she was dead, killed by those brutes. I could not leave: I could not stay," wailed Cawdor.

"Then Romla came down from the tree. She said she would perform the ceremonies of the dead for Zornova, after the fashion of the bison. So I left her with the body that had been Zornova and came here to wait," whispered Cawdor.

We were all stunned to silence. Zornova's sacrifice did not fit with our heroic visions of how our journey would turn out. We had gone another path while those dogs had nipped and then lunged at her with great ferocity, while she did nothing. We could not make sense out of this kind of death, this kind of useless sacrifice. Finally each of us came to realize that we had to accept Cawdor's story as the truth. After much biting and tearing of fur and flesh, great masses of dogs lunged as one and brought her down. Then they ripped her with their teeth and gnawed her flesh. As we listened, it was as though we became petrified. We were frozen and speechless in our grief. We remained motionless, unable to accept this unwanted ending to our saga. Until actual darkness descended upon us we remained emotionless as stone, but as the sun sank we relaxed somewhat and we wept within the anonymity of night.

Home

L OWERING CLOUDS enwrapped our joyless morning. We woke after fitful sleeping. None of us felt like moving. What were we to tell the others? How could we confess that we had let Zornova die for us? We had no answers for the questions that would surely maul our dreams. How could you slink away? Why did you do nothing to save her? We had no convincing answers. None of us had known the details of her plan. But none of us had forced her to tell us how things would work out in the end. Had each of us feared this pitiful ending? Had each of us chosen not to ask, not to know?

"We must go now," I said. "Zornova's sacrifice will have been wasted on us if we do not return home to those who wait for an answer from us."

"But I have no strength," whimpered Pabatackle.

"Blinkers is right, we must go," Wanda responded consolingly. "We must go tell all of the others of this great sacrifice by our leader. We must tell the story of this sacrifice; for this is the most important answer we have learned. Zornova has shown us that we must choose love and sacrifice over violence and hatred."

The rest of us nodded, knowing that Wanda was right. So we trudged ahead day after day, through falling snow, through wind and blizzards. We spent much of the time in silence, talking only when we must, for each of us was thinking about Zornova's choice. Each of us wondered if we could have given our life, as she had done. Could I make that choice? Each of us pondered this question.

We were caught off guard one day when Menke, the eagle, drifted through wind and snow.

"Welcome, oh weary ones, it is good that you return," he said. "Some had given up hope for you, then two weeks ago the strangest of things happened. Zornova began to appear to us in our dreams. She told us of what she had learned. She spoke, not always with the same words, but with the same intent. She told us that we must stop hating and start loving. Once she began to appear, we stopped our bickering and complaining, or at least most of it. Those who despaired, no longer despair. Those who had chosen to die have changed their minds and chose to live. But what I see now seems to confirm our fears, for not all of you are here. Save your story for later, for I can see that you are weary. I will send for the bison Tennial and Broken Horn to give you a ride the rest of the way back. Rest there among the trees and soon help will follow."

I will not bore you with all of the details of our return to Geyser District. Menki flapping her wings, flew off into the clouds and we took shelter under the trees overnight. Before noon the next day we heard the familiar thud of bison hooves and soon saw both Broken Horn and Tennial between the spruce branches.

"Welcome back," bellowed Broken Horn, "climb aboard quickly and we can be back home by nightfall."

It was a bumpy ride so most of our attention was given to holding on. Cawdor flew on ahead with Menki. As we got nearer to the meadow we heard the chitter chatter of many smaller and larger animals.

Morgorgor had food spread before us and we ate our first good meal in days. Though we were all weary from our travel we did manage to tell the assembled what we had learned.

"Well," I said, "we did not learn what we expected and the answers we received are not easy answers; they provide no quick solution to our problems. We learned that we must work together; we learned that we must look inside ourselves and ponder what the great power of the earth and sky has to tell us. This great power places within each of us the knowledge of what we must do. The great power is not remote, but close to us, surrounding us in all that we do. And, if we listen to the great power, it will tell us each what it has planned for us, and how we must live our lives. Zornova taught us this lesson, that love is more powerful than hate. She taught us that there are times when great sacrifices are needed. She saved us by sacrificing her life."

Wanda, who was now very weak and close to death, spoke softly, but firmly, "We must not forget Zornova's example; we must remind ourselves of both her love and her sacrifice."

"Yes, yes, we must remember," replied Morgorgor. "But we must let our weary travelers rest. Tomorrow we will celebrate the lessons we have been taught. We will celebrate the life of Zornova."

Wearily I crept back into the hollow log I had left months ago. No sooner had I curled up into a ball amongst the pine bows than I felt a warm furry critter against me. I could tell from the skunky smell that it was Rutorina. Oh well, I was too tired to care at the moment.

My dreams that night were varied. Sometimes, in my dreams, we fought off wild dogs, or we sped across the great clear lake in a motorboat, and at other times we raced along flooded streams or tried to outrun the animal control vans. But at least I slept deeply and well and long into the next day.

"Oh Blinkers," squeaked Rutorina, "you must wake up. It is almost time for the celebration."

As I rubbed the sleep from my eyes, I was glad to feel that much of my weariness had left me. I stretched, went outside into a snow-covered, sun-filled world. I followed Rutorina towards the center of the meadow where the celebration was to be held.

Though the bison Tennial was suffering the loss of his beloved Zornova, he spoke with dignity, "Come one and all as we celebrate the lives of those who have traveled far searching for the truth that has freed us from lethargy and despond. We thank the great power that has given us such great models for our lives. We thank the great power for providing us with such a beautiful place in which to live."

The celebration went on for the rest of the day and into the night. There were songs and dances, speeches, and, of course, there was much feasting. Great tributes were paid to all of us, but the highest honor was paid to Zornova. All of us were exhausted by the time the moon rose high in the sky. I headed back to my hollow log for a good night's sleep.

Much has happened in the months since that day of celebration. Wanda died of old age the next day. We both celebrated and mourned her passing. Romla returned two weeks later. She told us that Razor and the other dogs had returned to participate in Zornova's funeral. The dogs had decided, after witnessing Zornova's sacrifice, to turn away from their mean ways. In the springtime, after the winter snows had melted, Keeble returned, after wintering with the antelope. The ranger station for Geyser District has been re-built. I was asked to be the new ranger, but declined that honor, for I have not the bravery or dignity needed to fill that post.

Both the lands and the animals of the Geyser District are mostly healthy these days. There is talk of seeking to be reconciled with the humans, but we fear what might happen should we travel that road. So for now we think, we talk, we listen to the wind, to the streams, and to the voices of the earth for the wisdom of the one great power that pervades the earth and sky.